Sheldon pulled off her blazer, revealing a lacy black bra beneath. Instantly the men went wild and a million cameras flashed.

"Oh, this is great stuff for the Choo blog!" Jeff's sister Mercedes exclaimed as she dove into her purse for her digital camera.

Sheldon reached around behind her back and Jeff closed his eyes. In the middle of a strike demonstration in Times Square no less.

A huge cheer went up and Jeff opened his eyes.

There was Sheldon, surrounded by two thousand members of New York City's electricians union, holding the bra triumphantly above her head. Jeff knew exactly what they were thinking as they goggled her golden skin and perfect breasts. Breasts that made his mouth water.

And because of the press that he as a fabulous PR guy had supplied, invited actually, it was a picture that most of the world would see in tomorrow's papers.

Teasingly, Sheldon hollered, "You know, I gotta say, Jeff, this was a supergreat idea."

Blaze™

Dear Reader,

When I thought of the idea for this series, I originally imagined another heroine for Jeff, and saw Sheldon as nothing more than a plot diversion. But then two of my trusted friends told me that I *had* to make her the heroine, and these are *trusted* friends, so I really couldn't ignore them, thus, off I went. And something funny happened on the way—Sheldon became the perfect foil for Jeff.

As for the ending, one afternoon, while riding my bike in a nearby park, I figured out how it should happen. I began to cry as the scenes unfolded in my head, and I'm sure everyone in the park thought I was in the middle of some deep, traumatic turmoil! But that will be our secret...

I'd love to hear what you think of the story. Please write to Kathleen O'Reilly, P.O. Box 312, Nyack, NY 10989, or drop me an e-mail at kathleenoreilly@earthlink.net.

All the best,

Kathleen O'Reilly

BEYOND DARING
Kathleen O'Reilly

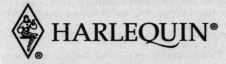

HARLEQUIN®

TORONTO • NEW YORK • LONDON
AMSTERDAM • PARIS • SYDNEY • HAMBURG
STOCKHOLM • ATHENS • TOKYO • MILAN • MADRID
PRAGUE • WARSAW • BUDAPEST • AUCKLAND

ISBN-13: 978-0-373-79313-6
ISBN-10:   0-373-79313-8

BEYOND DARING

www.eHarlequin.com

Printed in U.S.A.

ABOUT THE AUTHOR

Kathleen O'Reilly is the award-winning author of several romance novels. She enjoys pursuing her lifelong goal of sleeping late, creating a pantyhose-free work environment and entertaining readers all over the world. She lives in New York with her husband, two children and one rabbit. She loves to hear from her readers at either www.kathleenoreilly.com or by mail: P.O. Box 312, Nyack, NY 10960.

Books by Kathleen O'Reilly

HARLEQUIN BLAZE
297—BEYOND BREATHLESS*

HARLEQUIN TEMPTATION
967—PILLOW TALK
971—IT SHOULD HAPPEN TO YOU
975—BREAKFAST AT BETHANY'S
979—THE LONGEST NIGHT

*The Red Choo Diaries

1

JEFF BROOKS STOOD in his kitchen, furiously chopping green peppers, trying to expend some of the sexual frustration that currently had his shorts tied up in knots. Making breakfast was infinitely preferable than fantasizing about the woman happily snoozing in his bed.

Sheldon Summerville. Party girl. Socialite. Professional shopper. She was off-limits, with a capital *O*, little *f*, little *f. O-f-f. F-f-o.* He recited the jingle in his head, while thinking about her father, who, three months ago, had hired Jeff's firm to "redeem" her image. As if such a miracle could be performed by a mere mortal without the use of a padlocked chastity belt. Anything to shut down that perfect body, which she seemed determined to share with the world.

He selected an onion and began to hack, his eyes burning from the juices. Today he welcomed the discomfort. Sheldon Summerville left him frustrated professionally, sexually and mentally. He'd never met someone so determined to ignore what the world thought, especially her father, Wayne Summerville, the head of Summerville Consumer Products. They were the number two consumer product conglomerate in the world, proud maker of Toothbrite toothpaste, among other things.

Sheldon's party-girl reputation didn't sit well with Wayne's stockholders. Apparently, people with whiter teeth and fresh breath could be real frumps. However, even Jeff thought she went to extremes, and he was no monk himself.

The bigger mystery was why? No matter how long Jeff racked his brain, he couldn't figure Sheldon out, and she provided no hints. Always smiling in that vacant and clueless manner, which had ceased to fool him by Day Three. To make matters worse, she had no qualms about making lewd, yet majorly imaginative propositions—especially to him. He looked down at the mess he'd made of the onion and tossed the thing in the trash. Maybe shallots would be better.

Imaginative propositions he wanted to ignore. Propositions he should ignore. Okay, propositions that he didn't want to ignore….

Last night had been a stupid idea, but every night with Sheldon was a stupid idea. She had conveniently left him a message that she was going to the notorious club, Crobar. Jeff, knowing her message was code for multiple doses of alcohol, had shown up at ten, hoping to play responsible chaperone. At ten-oh-nine, he'd pulled her off the bartender, at ten-thirteen, he'd pulled her off the New York Ranger's goalie, and when he caught her kissing the bouncer, he knew it was past time for her to go home.

They'd argued until the cops came, threatening to arrest her, which would be exactly what she wanted. So Jeff had poured her into a taxi and taken her home. With him. It seemed like a good idea at the time. It had still seemed like a good idea six hours later when he woke up on his couch. In fact, it had seemed like such a great denouement, that he had congratulated himself on finally lassoing her into some sort of obedient servitude.

Everything had been fine until he opened the door to his bedroom, and saw her curled up, one hand cupped under her cheek like a child, sheets tangled between bare legs that were anything but childlike. Instantly his body moved to code red.

Jeff wasn't a self-disciplined man, had never worried about consequences, but this... The quiet little devil on his shoulder began whispering in his ear, telling him to go wake up her up in the best possible way. She wouldn't mind. Ah, there's the rub. She wouldn't mind. She would welcome him with arms wide open, those sea-blue eyes promising so many things. Glorious, wondrous things...

Thump. Thump. Thump. He whacked the shallots with his cleaver. Hard. Right now he needed to destroy something, and vegetables would be the victim of choice.

SLOWLY SHELDON SUMMERVILLE ROUSED herself from the fog of sleep into the fog that most people called life. She could smell him on the pillow, and she smiled, clutching it tighter to her. A persistent thump-thump echoed in the apartment, possibly the beating of her heart. Sunshine poured in through the window, and she stretched beneath the warm rays, her body sated...

Sated?

No, her body wasn't sated at all. There had been no touching, no kissing, nothing remotely sate-like last night. She merely slept in his bed. By herself.

So if he wasn't in his bed, where was he?

Sheldon threw back the covers, looked around, and then rubbed the sleep from her eyes. The mysterious thump-thump was consistent, and now that she knew it wasn't someone's heart, the sound was annoying.

Silently, she padded into the kitchen and watched him as he chopped, chef's knife in hand. Thump. Thump. Thump. First the green peppers, then back to the red ones. He didn't notice that she was standing, staring, ogling.

It was criminal that Jeff Brooks could be so tasty, so buff, yet still work in the stab-you-in-the-back-world of PR.

What was criminal was how badly she wanted him.

She pulled at her tank top and leaned back against the wall, adopting her patented vacant, though sexy stare. As soon as he felt the weight of her stare, he looked up, took a long eye-drinking of her skin, cocked one brow, and then went back to chopping peppers.

"Can you put some clothes on?"

Even his voice was sexy. Deep and rough, with that scuffed up mark of New York City, which he couldn't hide no matter how hard he tried. He was tall and lean, with strong legs emerging from the loose boxers that did more framing than concealing.

She soaked up the sight of him, her nipples hardening under the thin material, and without cold air, artificial device, and or a drenching of water.

Did he notice? No. He was happily making breakfast as if she didn't affect him at all.

Her mouth opened, so tempted to lash out at him, but it would ruin her image. Lashing out implied, passion, emotion, feeling. Instead, she leaned one hip against the edge of the granite counter, and let the full cascade of her platinum-blond hair fall over one well-formed breast.

From the time she was a kid, everything had been

done for her. All her whims had been granted, all her wants fulfilled. When you were the porcelain doll in the glass case, there was no reason for ambition or dreams.

You would think someone with her life would be happy and at peace, and if she were normal, that would probably have been the case. But there was something wrong with Sheldon, some piece of her wiring that never connected because she only felt empty. A tinman without a heart, a scarecrow without a brain and a lion without courage — all rolled into one.

The only tangible assets that belonged to Sheldon were a classically sculpted face and a body that made dead men moan. Hall of Famers is what the tabloids termed her cleavage and Sheldon had learned to use it whenever necessary.

Like now.

"You're *complaining?*" she drawled.

His strong, capable hands never stopped their mechanical chopping motion. For weeks, she'd had dreams of those hands on her. Steamy, vivid dreams that didn't disappear when she'd woken up.

"Not complaining, just trying to be helpful." He smiled at her, a toothy, advertising-type smile, possibly attributed to Toothbrite toothpaste. She suspected that he knew she hated it—both the toothpaste and the smile—which was why he did it.

"Is there something I can do?" she purred, her eyes gleaming when his hand stopped for a second.

He waved her off and continued working. "Hungover this morning?"

She pulled her hair into a ponytail, her chest lifting with the movement.

His gaze drifted down.

Her lips curved upward.

"Are you ever closed for business?" he asked.

Her eyes, normally vacuous and sultry, looked down meekly so that he wouldn't see the rage. Rage implied a depth that she didn't want to possess.

She backed away from the kitchen, the knife, and the man with the strong, capable hands, and padded barefoot across the room.

"I think I'll take a shower," she stated, slipping the tank over her head. It was a picture designed to freeze a man's brain, but he wasn't even watching. She was furious at herself for such an obvious act of desperation, but not so furious that she didn't slide the signature red panties down over her long, tanned legs as well.

"You don't mind do you?" she asked louder than necessary, her heart rapping inside her. He did this to her, reduced all her self-confidence to shreds.

Finally, his dark gaze lit over her, and she felt each and every white-hot touch. This time he didn't smile, only lowered his head and continued the whap-whap-whap against the cutting board.

Dismissed.

She left her clothes in a messy heap in the middle of the floor, and retreated to the loneliness of his shower. She turned on the warm spray and let it wash over her body, slipping between her breasts and thighs like a lover with knowing, capable hands. She shouldn't have been alone. He should be there, too.

Men didn't ignore her—ever. Especially men like Jeff. He was no extraordinary example of humanity. He was nice looking, with a hot body. But those dark, devilish eyes weren't supposed to be steely strong.

He should be weak.

Like her.

Men in the media business never had scruples. She was sure of it.

Life truly wasn't fair.

JEFF CONTINUED CHOPPING UNTIL all eleven green peppers had been diced into precise triangles. When there were no more peppers left to chop, he exhaled slowly, wiping the sweat from his forehead. It was a good thing she hadn't touched him because he knew in his heart, he would've jumped all over that.

He clicked on the television, letting the perky morning news shows dull the throbbing ache of his erection. An erection that needed to be inserted into the golden, shimmering skin that nestled beneath her thighs.

Brazilian. Why Brazilian?

Jeff groaned, loud, ragged. A rutting stag deprived of dinner. Would she notice if he spent the next thirty minutes jerking off? Probably. She'd want to help. That was her way.

He threw the peppers into the sauté pan and cranked up the gas burner, watching the thick skins pulse as the heat licked them into submission. Next he poured on the shallots, hacking off a chunk of butter, the butter sizzling from the burn. He took eight eggs from the refrigerator and kicked the door shut with extra force. It didn't help ease the pain, but these were desperate times that called for dramatic gestures, meaningless or not.

One by one he cracked the eggs, stirring them into a

fine glop before pouring over the tenderized vegetables. The heat of the flame melted the two mixtures into a fiery joining of culinary souls tasting the full extent of their passion.

Life really wasn't fair. He didn't want to want Sheldon. But there were parts of him that weren't cooperating. Parts of him that longed to be acquainted with parts of her.

Reacquainted. Because according to Little Miss "I Put My Body Where I Want To," said cock had already met said bare, naked nethers in a fiery joining of their own. Six weeks ago she'd claimed they'd had wild, untamed sex. Four times. And all he could remember was Sheldon trying to drink him under the table at Club Red. The rest of the night was a gut-rotting blank.

Expertly he flipped the omelet, shredding some Gouda over the smooth, golden body of the eggs.

Eventually, the cheese melted, sliding into each and every crevice of the sensual delicacy. Jeff flipped it onto a plate, ruthlessly sliced it into two halves, and then laid the plates on the bar.

When exposed to the sunlight, it looked liked nothing more than breakfast. His mind latched onto the commonplace thought, pushing aside visions of naked thighs and full breasts being drenched by the water from his shower. *Damn* it. He thought he was safe. Thought she'd given him a reprieve.

He was wrong.

Sheldon came into the living room, using a towel to dry the long lengths of her white-blond hair. The rest of her was still dripping wet. Nude—and dripping wet.

His eyes noticed, his hands began to shake, and his cock…well, at the moment he really didn't want to think about the tortured appendage that used to be functional.

She walked—*walked* being a very inadequate word to describe the sensual movement of her body—over to the small pile of underwear, picking up her bra and panties.

"Can't believe I was such a slob," she said, her eyes catching at the waistband of his boxers. "My, my, my…" she said, clicking her tongue against her teeth. He hated the celebration in her eyes, but he was a weakened piece of flesh. It was self-preservation alone that kept him motionless.

Her hand reached toward him, and he closed his eyes, steeling himself for her touch. He was strong. He was invincible. And mostly, there were ten million reasons that he could not touch her. Again.

"An omelet? You are talented," she whispered, her hand flirting near his waist. Yet, she didn't touch him.

He swallowed.

She noticed.

Her hand fell away, and he told himself that he was relieved, lying bastard that he was. But then, the gates of hell opened before him. She leaned down, the sweet angel of temptation, and touched the tip of her tongue to the engorged, pained, tortured while panting-like-a-happy-puppy tip of his cock.

She popped back up, wearing a smile of victory and nothing else. Then she wiggled her brows at him and strolled into the bathroom. He couldn't suppress his groan.

"I heard that," she yelled.

At the moment he didn't care.

SHELDON'S APARTMENT WAS ON THE Upper West Side.
Counting on the crosstown traffic, the trip would add an
extra forty-five minutes to his Monday morning com-
mute, but Jeff had no choice. It was time for a meeting
of the minds, simple as she pretended hers to be. He
hailed a cab and set her inside.

Firm and in control. He could handle it.

"New rules. No more nudity," he said, sliding in
beside her, keeping his voice low in case the cabbie had
big ears. Then he sliced his hand across his throat, just
in case she wasn't grasping the simplicity of his request.

Oh, she understood. She batted her eyelashes at him,
a gesture designed to hide the Einsteinian workings of
her brain. The simpleton act had never tricked Jeff, due
to the fact that he'd used it once or twice himself.

"What's wrong with the purity of the human body?
We're only animals at heart, Jeff."

"Don't get all Darwin on me, Sheldon. Keep the
clothes on. Keep the box closed."

Her mouth snapped together in a tight line. "You
think I'm a slut, don't you? You don't approve. Are you
a virgin, Jeff?"

He shot her a look. "You know I'm not. Don't you?"
he reminded her, because the absentee memory of the
night had eaten at him over the last few weeks. He
didn't forget sex. Ever. Even in the deepest lapses of
alcohol. *Ever.*

And with the one woman who had kept his cock throbbing in painful agony for what seemed like forever?

No way.

"Why does it matter if I have some fun?" she
asked, which on the surface was a perfectly logical,

rational question. However, Sheldon was neither logical, nor rational.

"I have a job to do, sweetheart. Your father is paying my firm large amounts of cash to keep you out of the papers. Nothing more. I'm going to do it, too."

She crossed her arms around her chest, not that he looked, and slumped back in the seat. "It always comes down to money, doesn't it?"

"Not always."

"Ha."

There was an edge in her voice, a pain that he'd never heard before. "What happened to you, Sheldon?"

"I use whatever I can to fight whoever I need to," she said, studying her nails.

The car slid to a screeching halt, smack in front of her building. Jeff paid the cabbie and told him to wait, he wasn't done with the lecture. He still had a good hour of diatribe left inside him.

They walked to the awning of her building, mere inches separating them, but the huge chasm loomed like an eroding fault line in the earth, just waiting to be split asunder.

"Why don't you stop fighting?" he asked, rubbing a hand over tired eyes. Playing bad-cop chaperone was exhausting and completely unrewarding.

She waved to her doorman, but stopped far enough away from the public eye. An unexpected moment of discretion. He was surprised. And pleased. "You want me. Why don't you stop fighting it?"

"I don't want you."

"Lying, much?"

"Keep the sex out of it."

Her eyes warmed, and then heated. "Kiss me, then. Just kiss me. No tongues, no bodies. Just two mouths touching."

He didn't want to kiss her, but she had laid down the challenge, and he would look spineless if he didn't comply.

So he kissed her. No tongues. No bodies. Just two mouths touching. Her lips were soft and pliable, and so was the look in her eyes. There wasn't the usual vacancy in her gaze. Shockingly, there was innocence there. Vulnerability. Qualities he couldn't pin on Sheldon if he tried. But there they were. Staring him in the face.

His first instinct was to run. He even turned to go.

"You shouldn't fight it," she whispered.

"Go inside."

She started to argue, but maybe she saw the pleading in his eyes, maybe she saw the battered animal that lurked inside him, maybe she was just tired. It didn't matter, she smiled at the doorman, and blithely went on her way.

And Jeff felt himself breathe again.

He returned to the curb, only to find his cabbie had disappeared, probably hoping to find an even bigger sucker than Jeff.

Even cabbies had their dreams.

COLUMBIA-STARR COMMUNICATIONS OCCUPIED a sophisticated floor of offices near Midtown. Lots of red and black and polka dots and flash. It was the hottest PR firm in New York—at least it was right now, and Jeff considered it quite the achievement that he'd landed the job all on his own.

He pulled open the glass doors and was immediately

greeted by a strange man sitting behind what used to be his secretary's desk.

"Mr. Summerville called. He'll be here in ten."

"Who are you?" asked Jeff.

"Phil Carter. Rent-a-temp. Nice tie, by the way," he said, a glint in his eye.

Oh, joy. Jeff had a very modern attitude toward alternative lifestyles, but it was nine-thirty in the morning, and he didn't like men who dressed better than he did. "Let me begin with, you're fired."

"Hello, Mr. Ego has arrived! They warned me about you."

"Are you always like this?"

Phil balanced his face on his hands, smiling like an imp. A very gay imp, but an imp. Then he began to sing. "I gotta be me. I gotta be me."

"Enough. You know the software we use?"

"You betcha."

"Good speller, impeccable grammar?"

"Philistine. *P-h-i-l-i-s-t-i-n-e.* Participle phrases are used chiefly to modify nouns, but a dangling participle is confusing to the reader. For example, 'Sitting on his ass, the bird flew by the window.'"

Just then the phone rang.

"Phone manners?" barked Jeff.

Phil pushed a button on the phone and started speaking into his headset. "Columbia-Starr Communications. Mr. Jeff Brooks's office. How may I help you?" Phil frowned ominously. "Mr. Brooks did what? And then the cops told him what? And now the Smoking Gun wrote what? No comment. And that's my final comment. Thank you for calling Columbia-Starr Communications. Shaping The World, A Million Minds At A Time. Have a nice day."

Phil hung up and gave Jeff an expectant look.

Okay, the guy was good, better than the last four temps he'd had. Jeff looked down at the phone. "Who was that?"

"Your mother. Baked ziti at her apartment Wednesday at eight."

It was too much to comprehend after four hours of restless sleep, and a hard-on that was now mummified permanently. "What about all the other stuff you were saying? With the cops?" The last thing he needed was more Sheldon-fodder for the rags.

Phil wiggled his index finger. "Fastest mute finger in the West."

Jeff nodded. "Okay, you pass. I like my coffee black," he ordered, taking off for the zen-like quiet of his office.

"No sugar?" yelled Phil.

Jeff slammed the door.

"Savage!"

JEFF'S HEADACHE WAS JUST beginning to recede when the intercom buzzed.

"A Mr. Summerville is waiting for you, Mr. Brooks. Should I show him in?"

Sheldon's dad. Quickly, Jeff flipped through the morning trade rags to see what sort of lies, half truths and full truths were being written about her.

The Post mentioned her makeout session with the goalie. *The Daily News* listed a Sheldon-sighting at Crobar, but it wasn't too bad. All in all, they'd written tons worse about Sheldon before.

Only two items today. Maybe her father would be happy.

Thirty seconds later, Wayne Summerville was in his office.

"What the hell am I paying you for, boy?"

Okay, not happy. Jeff forced a smile. "There's the blind item on Page Six about the wayward socialite that's been giving large amounts of cash to the homeless."

"That's not my daughter," he said, leaning over Jeff's desk, probably so Jeff could feel the full force of his anger.

Check. Anger felt.

"It might not be, Wayne, but people could assume it is. That's the beauty of blind items. We can plant something with the Daily Dish tomorrow."

"Jeff, now listen. I like you, boy. Really do. But your firm is charging me an obscene amount of money to transform my daughter's image into something more palatable to our stockholders. And do you know what's happened to my daughter's image since I hired you?"

Jeff stared into the dark dredges of his Columbia-Starr Communications coffee cup. "What, sir?"

"I didn't think it could happen. Truly didn't believe it could happen, but her image has gotten worse. Gone right in the toilet."

"Your daughter's a rather headstrong young lady." It was an understatement from a man well-versed in overstatements.

"Then get tough, Jeff. I want to announce her engagement in three months, and when she's off swapping spit and who knows what other bodily fluids with a bartender at some newfangled club in the Meatpacking District, it's not going to happen."

Jeff lifted his head and backtracked for a moment. "What engagement? A marriage engagement?"

"Sure. Sheldon's marrying the heir to Con-Mason U.S.A. We're signing all the papers in a few weeks." Wayne rubbed his hands together. "It'll be the biggest merger this side of the Mississip since Exxon-Mobil. Course that'd be west of the Mississip. Damn, it'd be the biggest merger in this whole gosh-darned country."

"She knows this?"

"The merger?"

"The marriage?" asked Jeff, frowning.

"Sure. Joshua's a presentable boy, Harvard grad, one of the cities most eligible bachelors, and we've had a long talk. Right proud of my little girl."

"An engagement," muttered Jeff. This wasn't the Dark Ages where women were forced to submit to the whims of men. At least, in most cases.

"It's a win-win for everybody. Sheldon gets more money than God and the devil combined. Summerville CP gets expansion into the Chinese markets that Con-Mason's already has such a lock on. And best of all, there'll be no taxes to pay on the stock swap because of the laws of this fine country that protect the sacred union between a man and his wife. God bless the USA."

Jeff felt the urge to cross himself but refrained because he didn't think Wayne would see the humor.

"I'll do better, sir. Now that I have a full understanding of the situation, I'm sure Sheldon and I can work something out," he said earnestly, all while subversive ideas were buzzing around in his head.

Yeah, he'd talk to her. He could rescue her. Explain to her the options she had. Jeff choreographed the entire scene, heroic orchestration playing in the background. Close up to her sea-blue eyes as she stared at him worshipfully.

Jeff smiled to himself.

"And I've got an incentive for you, Jeff. Sort of my way of insuring that we all succeed. When the merger happens between Con-Mason U.S.A. and Summerville CP, we're going to need a firm to do all our public relations work. Never believed in trying to do that sort of thing in-house, better to let the pros handle it. And I think Columbia-Starr Communications would be right perfect. Course, then they'd have to call it Columbia-Starr-Brooks Communications. Sounds nice, don't you think? Just like heavenly bells to a man's ear."

Then Wayne grinned at Jeff, his sea-blue eyes long faded to dollar-sign green.

And thus, Jeff was slapped back into the coffee-cup dregs of his reality. The world of Sheldon Summerville was a gold-studded planet, a monied universe. Wayne Summerville bought companies over breakfast and Jeff Brooks saved up eight long years for a boat. Tomorrow's disillusions were today's grand illusions. In his business, Jeff had to be careful not to believe his own spin.

He examined the Columbia-Starr logo, thinking that maybe there was a place for Brooks on the coffee cup, too.

The heroic orchestrations playing in his head screeched to a full stop, and the picture of Sheldon's sea-blue eyes, once lit with heroic worship, faded to black.

Like that would ever happen anyway.

2

THERE WAS ONLY ONE PERSON that Jeff depended on for advice. Himself. However, when gazillion-dollar financial matters were involved, he was out of his league, although he'd never admit it to anybody, especially his older brother, Andrew.

And it was for this reason that, when he called Andrew to meet him for happy hour, he told his brother that he needed to hit him up for money for a charitable donation.

Andrew was a successful hedge-fund manager—a hugely successful hedge-fund manager.

Jeff tried not to compare his successes to Andrew's, because he'd always come up short—several billion short, in case anyone was counting. Of course even God couldn't really compare to Andrew's successes. But to be fair, God took a day off once a week, and Andrew never did. Jeff was a firm believer in a day off.

"So, what's this cause of yours?" asked Andrew, sitting at the bar, sipping on his beer.

"Heart disease in kids. We're doing a campaign to raise awareness. There's some great breakthroughs in the medical community, new drugs that are entering trials and we're putting together a complete media package, kicking off with this Their Hearts On The Line campaign. Great stuff. Really hits you right here," said Jeff, laying a hand over his chest.

"How much do you need?"

"What's the life of a child worth to you, Andrew? Then multiply that by fifty."

"That's serious cash."

"Heart disease is serious business."

"All right," said Andrew, who then wrote one very large check.

Jeff tucked the paper in his pocket; he'd mail it to a charity tomorrow. He loved his brother unconditionally, owed him in ways that he could never pay back, but sometimes a man had to have a little fun. Separating Andrew from his vault full of money was Jeff's favorite game. In the old days, those checks would be made out to Jeff, but eventually Jeff had managed on his own, so he had to think of new, better and more philanthropic causes for Andrew's millions.

As the checks had gotten bigger, Andrew developed a reputation as a high roller within charity circles, and Jeff got to watch the pained expression on Andrew's face as he signed his name at the bottom of each and every one.

Life didn't get any better than this.

"So, how're you doing?" asked Jeff. "How's the new firm?"

"Lots of work," said Andrew, blowing out a breath. "But worth it."

"Saw where Jamie made the cover of *Forbes*."

"Yeah," said Andrew. At the mention of his girlfriend, Andrew's face reflected something approaching humanity. *Whatever.*

Jeff leaned against the bar and spotted a brunette

watching him over the rim of her glass. Automatically he smiled at her, because deep in his genetic makeup, Jeff was wired for one thing: sex.

Andrew watched the interplay but didn't say anything. He didn't have to, his eyes said it all. Andrew disapproved of Jeff's lifestyle. *Big whoop.*

"I got a call from Ed Weinberger at Stockard-Vine Public Relations. We played on a golf foursome a while back. Anyway, he had a question about some stock, and I mentioned you to him. Turns out they're looking for a VP. You should think about it."

Jeff frowned into his beer mug. That was the problem with being around Andrew. His brother reminded him of the other thing that existed beyond sex and Jeff's boat fund: responsibilities, with a capital *R*. The brunette stopped her perusing, and Jeff took a long swallow of beer. Responsibilities were best taken on when drunk.

Eventually, the taste of the lager left his mouth, but the sour taste of life remained.

Jeff met his brother's eyes squarely. "Andrew, I'm not eighteen anymore. I have a career and a job that I got all by myself. I don't need your help."

Someday, his brother might understand that Jeff wanted to make it solo. 'Course, Andrew would probably be dead before it all sunk it, but Jeff would keep reminding him.

They'd been raised without their father, and Andrew had taken care of the Brooks family for so long that sometimes he forgot that everyone could take care of themselves now.

"I know you don't like my help. I'm just letting you know the possibilities are there. It'd get you one step closer to that boat you want."

Now it was time to change the subject. "So, listen, I have a question for you," started Jeff, picking up a handful of peanuts and lining them up on his napkin.

"Shoot."

"When you need to get somebody in line with your way of thinking, what do you do?"

"You're kidding me. I thought you were the PR whiz."

Damn. Lack of sleep was causing Jeff to lose his touch. "This really isn't a PR sort of question. It's more a question of mankind," said Jeff, popping a peanut in his mouth and chewing thoughtfully.

"Or womankind?"

"I don't think we need to be gender-specific here. I've been thinking about this. I mean, PR is my business and all, but there are more important things going on in the world, and I need to pay attention to them."

"What's her name?"

"You know, it really ticks me off that you have such a low opinion of me that you think if I'm having issues, it has to be about women. I have thoughts. Deep thoughts."

"Usually involving sex."

"You don't see my sex life thrown out onto the Internet like some cheap *Playboy* movie of the week," Jeff reminded him.

Andrew's face closed off. "That's not fair."

It probably wasn't, but that never stopped Jeff. Last fall, Andrew and Jamie's affair had been loosely fictionalized all over America in Andrew and Jeff's younger sister's sex blog. Gotta love technology.

"And it's not fair that you don't give me credit for deeper character virtues. You think all I have on the brain is women and sex."

"What did you do last night?" asked Andrew.

"I was at a club."

"By yourself?"

"There's lots of people at clubs."

"The night before?"

"I don't think that matters."

"Another club?"

"Maybe."

"And did you get laid on either one of these two nights?"

Ah, moral dilemma. Jeff could admit the truth—tell his brother that he'd been celibate for the past three months, except for the one night of sex with Sheldon that he couldn't remember. That'd be the answer from a man with deeper character virtues.

The alternative would be to lie about his current sexual endeavors, or lack thereof, because Andrew would never believe that Jeff wasn't hitting the sheets with somebody—anybody, for that matter.

"Duh. 'Course I got laid," said Jeff, rolling his eyes.

"I rest my case," replied Andrew, raising his glass.

"You tricked me!" exclaimed Jeff, using his inherited acting skills to fake indignation.

Andrew gave him The Look.

Jeff blew out a breath.

Now that was out of the way, too.

On to the one question that had been burning in Jeff's brain.

"Listen, I need to ask you a hypothetical question. What would happen if there was a merger between Con-Mason U.S.A. and Summerville Consumer Products?"

Andrew whistled. "No shit?"

"I said hypothetical."

Andrew stared up at the ceiling, lips pursed. Andrew thought this was his thinking look.

Jeff called it the Stick-Up-My-Ass look.

"Okay, Con-Mason—Chinese. Summerville—rumors of new product development." He looked back at his brother. "All in all, big. Very, very big. But what does Con-Mason get out of this?"

Sheldon. "My lips are sealed," answered Jeff. "So this would be huge? Worth lots of money?"

"Many zeroes, Jeff. More than you can count."

That's what Jeff was afraid of. Time to cut off moronic heroic notions before said notions rose up to bite him in the butt.

"So, when are you going to propose to Jamie?" asked Jeff, expertly steering the conversation into friendlier waters.

Andrew's face turned a whiter shade of pale. "That's a big step."

"Chicken?"

"No, it's just that a man needs to think of his life strategically. One step at a time. You start with your business goals, get those in order and then move on to personal ones. Jamie and I will end up married, but I want to get the new firm right up there in the top two."

"You mean the top ten?"

"Uh, no, the top two."

"And then, after many years have passed, and you're both old and gray? You try and get down on one knee to propose, but by this time you're arthritic in not only one, but both knees, and she has to help you up. What if she's not going to wait for you,

Andrew? What if she's not going to wait for you to achieve your goals?"

Jeff knew that Jamie would wait on Andrew forever if necessary, but Jeff thought it'd be more fun to put the fear of loneliness into his brother. Jamie would thank him for it later.

"Of course she'll wait until the firm is ready. Jamie's more ambitious than I am," said Andrew, traces of doubt coloring his voice.

Jeff covered his smile with a hand to his face and then put on a serious look. "If you really want something, you have to put everything aside, don't you?" Secretly, Jeff had always admired Andrew's single-minded focus. Andrew never let the distractions of life get in his way. If Jeff had been that single-minded, it would be Columbia-Starr-Brooks Communication by now, and he'd be the proud owner of a sweet thirty-five-foot double-masted sailboat with polished decks. Pipedreams was what he used to call his goals. But now they seemed within reach. Maybe he could be more like Andrew…

Jeff looked at Andrew with new respect. Well, technically, he'd always respected his brother, but he usually hid it. This time he didn't.

"You apply yourself, put in the hours, and it'll pay off in the end. Life works out, Jeff. It always does."

Yeah, life would work out for everyone but Sheldon. "No matter if you don't exactly agree with what's going on?"

Andrew nodded wisely, his brow furrowed. "Let me tell you a secret, Jeff. Corporate America is not for the faint of heart. It's a tough, bullshit business, where money trumps all else. It's not going to change. You'll come across a lot of times where you don't agree with what's going on. But that's the way business works. The people who own the company decide how they're going to run it, and they don't care about you. So if you want something, you get it. End of story. Haven't you learned anything from me?"

"Sure" said Jeff, popping a peanut in his mouth. "Apply yourself, focus, ignore the crap. I can do that."

Maybe.

WHEN JEFF HAD CALLED SHELDON to say he wanted to meet with her on Thursday, Sheldon knew the perfect place. Agent Provocateur was stylish but lurid, in a genitalia-engorging way. By the time Jeff made it through the door at the Soho shop, Sheldon was wielding eight transparent teddies, three sheer bras and one garter belt complete with little black bows. He stopped and stared. Suddenly, he was a man traveling in another dimension, a dimension not only of sight and sound, but of sheer lace and peek-a-boo bras. Next stop, the Erection Zone.

Sheldon held up a bra with cut-out nipples and smiled. "What do you think?"

His Adams apple bobbed up and down. That firm yet classical mouth pulled into a frown. His sexy brown eyes were full of foreboding, yet flavored with the tastiest bit of lust. "I thought we had a new set of ground rules."

"You said no nudity." With garments in hand, she strolled to the dressing rooms. "This isn't nudity. Coming?"

He followed her, but when it came to breaching the sanctity of the changing room, he stopped at the door, crossing his arms over his chest. "I'll wait."

She sighed. "Whatever."

Inside, she stripped off her clothes and pulled on the white lace teddy. "What did you want to talk to me about?"

"I know why you're doing this."

Sheldon paused. "Doing what?"

"This whole vamp-the-world thing."

She giggled. *Vamp* was such a cute, old-fashioned word, and Jeff was so—not. Unless she missed her guess, and she never did, that suit was Armani. No, the man didn't have an old-fashioned bone in his body as hard, muscular and top-shelf as that body was. "Why am I vamping the world?"

"Your father told me about the engagement."

Now that stopped her cold. For only a second. Then she pasted the smile back on her face and began to tie the little white straps that kept the top in place. Sheldon looked in the mirror, pleased with the way her breasts nearly spilled over the cups. The white was innocent and classy, but the whole ensemble screamed "Take me, I'm yours."

"What about it?" she asked in a bored voice.

"You don't want this to happen."

Sheldon opened the door and watched his face turn a pleasant shade of bone-white that went well with his dark hair. "Grow up, Jeff," she told him, then performed a sexy little turn. "What do you think?" she asked, cocking a hand on her hip, making sure he could appreciate the curve of her rear.

"It's nice," he said, swallowing. He dragged his gaze up and focused on the wall. "You're okay with the marriage thing, then?"

She took a step closer, letting lace-covered nipples brush against his chest, as much for her as for him. "I live in a separate place from most of the rest of the world. I can't marry just anybody. There're family considerations, corporate considerations and genetic considerations."

"You're making that up," he accused, his eyes straying to her cleavage.

Sheldon faced the mirror and pulled at one strap, letting it hang off her shoulder. "The genetic considerations aren't true, but the rest is. It's a trade-off, Jeff. I get what I want, and Daddy gets what he wants. What could be better?"

This time his gaze locked onto her face, trapping her there. "What do you want, Sheldon?"

She looked away, deciding she didn't like the innocent white look on her. No, she needed something with spice. Black. Or her signature red. That would complement her blond hair, not wash it out. "That's for me to know and you to speculate on for the rest of your days."

"So you're going to go through with this?"

"Uh, yeah."

"You're sure?"

"Do I need to repeat myself?"

"Well, you do seem to favor a lot of guys for a woman who's about to get married."

"It's not like it's going to happen next week."

"And you're sowing your wild oats?"

She tilted her head. "Absolutely."

"And that's your final answer?"

"Yeah, Reege."

She thought he would argue more. Secretly, she wanted him to argue more, but instead he sighed, giving up on her. "Okay, then we've got lots of work to do, but if we focus, we're cool. I've come up with a five-point plan strategically designed to fix your image."

She slammed the door in his face and stripped off the teddy. "I don't need to *fix* my image."

"You do if you're going to go through with this," he answered matter-of-factly.

She flung open the door, because she hated the cool, matter-of-fact tone he used. This was her life he wanted to fix, as if she were some chipped statue, or a knockoff purse with a broken zipper.

"You said no nudity," he reminded her.

She slammed the door shut. "No, *you* said that."

"But you promised."

"Fine," she said, picking out the demi-bra and garter belt. "Tell me about this brilliant plan of yours," she said, sliding on a pair of red panties, gritting her teeth the whole time.

"Okay. There're five basic areas that we can target— personal life, artistic endeavors, sports, giving back to the community and what I call the "little man.""

Giving back to the community? The "little man"?

Sheldon pulled on the hose, nearly running them, and then snapped the demi-bra in place. "You've given this a lot of thought."

"It's my job."

"Of course," she said, and examined herself in the mirror.

Artistic endeavors? What a crock. She'd show him artistic endeavors. She pulled the bra cup down half an inch, exposing one nicely artistic nipple. Then she opened the door. "Should I get this one?"

He didn't move.

She waved a hand in front of his face. "Jeff?"

He gave his head one hard shake. "You are so paying for this, Sheldon."

"For what?"

He pulled at the bra cup, covering her up, but she didn't miss the way his thumb lingered.

"Nothing," he answered. "All we need to do is focus."

Focus. He thought they needed to focus. She *knew* they needed to have sex. Mad, passionate, glorious sex so that she could exorcise Jeff Brooks from her system before he "fixed" her.

Sheldon went back into the dressing room and pulled on her sundress and sandals, a pleased smile on her face as she remembered the feel of his hands on her. Outside the door, she could hear his pacing. All that restrained tension.

Someday. Someday soon, Jeff Brooks.

Yeah, Sheldon knew exactly what she wanted.

3

THE SUMMERVILLE ENCLAVE WAS situated overlooking the ocean in the Hamptons. Sheldon had spent every single weekend of her summers there, and the smell of the sea air never failed to stir her senses. The sun was setting over her shoulder, casting a glimmering reflection on the water.

There was something about the solitude of the water that called to her. It was a time when she could turn off all the extraneous aspects of the Summerville legacy— of which there were many—and simply be.

As she sat on the boat dock, watching the gray waters of the Atlantic, she took another deep breath. A seagull perched on a wooden post, waiting for bread crumbs. He'd be waiting for a long time because Sheldon wasn't the bread crumb type.

Being a Summerville had its privileges, that was for sure. She could jet off to Aspen or the Alps, take off for the Caribbean whenever she got the urge and could spend three times the GNP of Cuba on clothes.

It'd be really, really petty to complain, so she didn't. She rose and took a few steps closer to the water, the catamarans lazily riding the swells, the gentle lapping of the waves soothing her nerves, clearing her head of all negativity.

Sometimes she thought she should be doing something meaningful with her life. But then she'd go out and tie one on and would eventually come to the realization that there were people in the world destined for meaningful things.

Sheldon wasn't one of them.

She spotted her sister, Cami, leaving the house, walking down the steps toward Sheldon. As if she needed a reminder of her place in the grand scheme of things.

Camille Summerville, at age twenty-four, was two years younger than Sheldon and a paler, more refined version of her sister. Sheldon still loved her in spite of it. Cami didn't have the flash of Sheldon, she wore khakis and linen shirts and she gardened. As she walked out on the beach, her sneakers kicked in the sand. Another difference—Sheldon wouldn't be caught dead in sneakers.

"I'm supposed to tell you that dinner will be served at seven," said Cami.

"Yeah, sounds great."

"Monique called an hour ago, and left a message. She wants you to go out with some of her friends."

Monique was their mother's tennis coach, Sheldon barely knew her. "What now?"

"I don't know, but she kept talking about some tennis tournament."

"I don't play tennis."

"I think she's angling for someone to sponsor her," admitted Cami.

"Why can't people just come out and ask? Why pretend to be friends, or to be nice, or to be interested in anything about me? Why not just be honest?"

"Don't shoot me, I'm just the service."

Sheldon laughed. "I don't believe that no one ever hits you up for stuff. Use your influence, Sheldon," she said in a mocking voice.

"I solved that a long time ago."

"How?"

"I told them that Dad gave it all to you. I'm the poor, struggling medical student."

Sheldon swung a mock fist, and Cami dodged. Somehow Cami always managed to escape.

This time her sister gave her a sympathetic look. "The Conrads will be here, too. You should wear something nice. Dad would like that."

"Yeah, I will. I thought you were in the city for the weekend."

Cami was finishing up her second year of medical school at Columbia and never had time off, summers included. Cami was destined for meaningful things.

"I should be. Got the boards to study for, but I needed to talk to you." She stuffed her hands in her pockets and bit her lip, looking majorly guilty.

"What about?" asked Sheldon, curious about what sort of thing would give Cami a guilt complex. A *B-* on a test? A parking ticket? Walking past a homeless guy on Tenth Avenue without throwing money in his direction?

"I want to go to the islands this weekend, and I need you to cover for me."

And no, it wasn't anything wicked at all. Cami just wanted a break. "Why can't you tell Mom?"

"Two reasons. One, she'd give me serious grief for skipping out on my studies. And two, Lance. She thinks it's a 'rebellious phase' I'm going through."

"Lance?"

Cami's faced turned all dreamy, and she let out one of those long, seventh-grade sighs. "Lance. He's a drummer in this band." Cami looked around to see if anyone else was listening. Satisfied that the bird wasn't going to tell, she continued. "We're gonna do it, Sheldon."

"Have sex?"

"Heck, no, we've done that hundreds of times. We're going to go away for a weekend. And I want to skinny dip in the ocean and have sex on the beach and do all those crazy tropical things that normal people are rumored to have done. Have you ever had sex on the beach?"

Actually, Sheldon hadn't because the beach was her place and her place alone. But Cami looked all goo-goo about the prospect, so Sheldon put on her best "dreamy-flashback" smile. "It's great. It's really hot, and you get all sweaty and sticky, but then, just when you think it's totally yuck, you can dive into the ocean and cool off, the warm waters wrapping around you. Five stars, Cami. Definitely."

"Oh, I can't wait. And I bought a new bikini. With strings."

"You and Lance will have a great time."

Playfully, Sheldon kicked some sand in Cami's direction. Sheldon didn't have any of Cami's important things to worry about. Yeah, no muss, no guilt. Until the day she was engaged, she was as free as the bird still perched nearby, waiting patiently for crumbs.

Sheldon fished in her pocket and tossed the bird an Altoid's mint. Not a piece of bread, but he'd have great breath. He flew down and picked up the mint.

Cami shook her head.

"You know, you and Josh should get married in the Caribbean. Barefoot. Maybe some quiet guitar music in the background. What do you think?"

"Yeah, maybe," answered Sheldon. "Let's go inside. After all, don't want to keep Josh waiting."

THE FORMAL DINING ROOM SEATED forty when necessary. Tonight the table was set for eight, but Sheldon really wished they'd put in the extra leaves so that conversation would be kept to a minimum.

The four extra seats were occupied by the Conrad family: James Conrad, his wife, Marge; their daughter, Jennifer; and the favored son, Josh, Sheldon's soon to be fiancé.

She picked at her peas and watched Josh from the corner of her eye. He was handsome, with sun-bleached California hair, earnest blue eyes, a dimple in his chin and a mouth that was a hair too wide, but it fit him. Josh was the eternal optimist. For some reason, every time Sheldon laid eyes on him, she wanted to kill him. Not the best start for a marriage.

"Sheldon, how's your steak, honey?"

Sheldon smiled at her father. "I think I'm going to become a vegetarian. Do you know how they make steak? Cutting up the cows, all that blood—"

Sheldon's mother held up a perfectly manicured hand. "Not at the dinner table, Sheldon."

Sheldon blinked vacantly. "Sure, Mom."

Her mother, ever the peacemaker, turned to Josh. "So, Josh, what's new and exciting at Con-Mason?"

He speared a piece of meat with his fork, his mouth curved into an even bigger smile than usual. "Sales for the new line of bathroom cleaners are up seventeen percent, and we've put some incentives in place for the sales team. Very exciting stuff. I think third quarter growth will surprise everyone—especially the analysts." Then he took a bite of his steak and chewed. Still smiling.

"Isn't that nice?" Sheldon's mother, Cynthia, looked every bit the Hamptons matron. Golden blonde, tanned and still gorgeous. That would be Sheldon in about twenty years, although Cynthia was missing Sheldon's vacant expression. Her mother actually cared about things.

Then Cynthia turned to her oldest daughter. "Isn't that nice, Sheldon?"

"Better than nice, Mom." She looked in Josh's direction. "Nuclear."

He met her eyes, smiled, and then went back to his dinner. Oh, yes, theirs would be a match made in heaven.

The dinner conversation followed a well-established order. Gossip, excluding the Summerville and Conrad families, of course. Next up was the polo season. No one at the table played, including Josh, who was a golfer like Sheldon's dad. However, lack of participation never stopped a heated discussion about how disappointing last season was.

Over dessert, Marge Conrad and Cynthia would launch into a full critique of the fall fashion season, each woman bemoaning her loss of figure. Both were size four.

Scintillating stuff, and after twenty-six years of it, Sheldon knew it all by heart.

After the last of the plates had been cleared away, her father opened a bottle of wine, pouring everyone a glass. Then he moved to stand behind her, his hands on her shoulders. "I have an announcement to make. I think y'all are going to be seeing a new side of Sheldon. Gave me a big surprise when she came to me and talked about expanding her world. Giving back to the community, trying artistic endeavors, taking an interest in New York's fine array of sports offerings, turning her personal life into something more meaningful. I was tickled pink. And then, she told me about her favorite idea, sticking up for the 'little man.'" He raised a glass. "To Sheldon, apple of my eye and owner of my heart."

Sheldon raised her glass, pasting a smile on her face. So Jeff was that confident of his five-point plan that he'd pitched it to her father like a new advertising slogan?

Rage burned inside her, an oddly unfamiliar emotion. She'd be damned if Jeff was going to treat her like dish-washing powder.

Maybe she had a meaningless existence, maybe she was a black hole of humanity, but this time he had pushed her too far. This was a new and improved Sheldon with extra strength for tackling stubborn PR flacks where they lived.

Little did he know it, but Jeff Brooks had just issued a declaration of war.

MERCEDES BROOKS WAS JEFF'S younger sister and partner in crime, usually against Andrew. Then, when they were done with that, they'd turn on each other in that genuine, loving yet exquisitely painful sibling way that had endured since the dawn of time.

If she'd been homely or fat, Jeff might have cut her some slack, but Mercedes had looks. Not model looks, like Sheldon, but she had a unique I-can-kick-your-ass glint in her eyes that seemed to drive guys wild.

Jeff, having been the recipient of said glint more than once, was immune.

Currently, his pain-in-the-butt sister was curled up in his office, hogging his favorite chair, reading the *New York Times*—not her usual reading material. She pushed her dark hair out of her eyes and continued to bitch. Another one of Mercedes' finer qualities.

She pointed to the article she was reading and scowled. "I don't think sex is cheapening America, do you?"

"What?" asked Jeff, the word *sex* capturing his interest.

"They're talking about my blog."

"Oh," muttered Jeff, going over his notes. Mercedes had a sex blog that she wrote anonymously. *The Red Choo Diaries.* Most of his friends' sisters wrote their secrets in their diaries. Not Mercedes. No, the whole freaking world had to know about her secrets.

"I don't have time for this, Mercedes," he said, sending off an e-mail to a reporter at the *Daily News,* his last reminder before today's event.

"Why not? Don't you care about the freedom of the press? You, of all people, who depend on the media in order to do your job? I think you're a traitor in disguise, Jeff. I can't believe you're my brother.

"Oh, calm down, Mercedes. You write a sex blog, not *Gone with the Wind.*"

"And isn't it a fact that you lie, cheat and brainwash people for a living?"

"On a good day, yes."

She humphed and went back to the paper. "The least you could do is help me write an Op-Ed piece. You know, something with a great hook and pizzazz. I need to work on my platform."

"What platform?" he asked.

"A marketing platform. My agent told me that."

Jeff frowned. "What agent?"

"Do you pay attention to anything I tell you?"

"No."

"At least Andrew listens to me."

"I got him the other day."

That brought the joy back into Mercedes's eyes. "Really? How?"

"I told him that Jamie wouldn't wait forever for him to propose."

"Oh, what did he do? Pale, pasty complexion, the eye dodge, or the back-brace-posture-pose."

"All of the above."

"I bet he proposes next week."

"Nah, three months. At his heart, Andrew's too conservative."

"With Jamie? Hello! They played hide the salami in a *limo*. On a *workday*. We have to bet. One thousand dollars says he proposes within the month."

"You don't have a thousand dollars to lose, Mercedes. You quit your job as a real journalist, who knows why."

Mercedes gave a careless shrug. "It was too structured. I felt like the paper limited my creative endeavors. I'm an artist."

"And as an unemployed artist, you don't have one thousand dollars to lose."

"Do too. Got my first advance check the other day."

"Advance for what?"

"My book deal."

"You sold a book?"

"I told you," she started, then noticed the smile on his face. "You're such a jerk."

"A thousand dollars? You're on."

Mercedes laughed. "Putting your money where your mouth is, big boy?"

"'Course I'm in."

"Now you have to help me write the essay."

"Can't right now. Have to meet Sheldon at the electricians' strike."

Her eyes skimmed over him, for the first time taking in the faded blue jeans, the Rolling Stones T-shirt. "A strike? What the heck are you doing on a picket line? They fired you at Columbia-Starr didn't they, and you've got this new secret career and never told us. Andrew is going to love this mess, Jeff. I can hear the lectures already."

"Nice try. It's for the job."

"Columbia-Starr is representing the union?" she asked, raising her eyebrows.

"It's not that far-fetched, but no. I'm working on Sheldon Summerville's image. She's going to go out on the picket line and walk it for a bit."

Mercedes began to laugh. "You're kidding me, right?"

"No, it's part of a new plan to redesign her image."

"And she's okay with this?"

"'Course," he said, although he wasn't exactly sure she was okay with it. In fact, he suspected that she was not okay with it, but she seemed to be going along with his ideas. So, uh, she must be okay with it.

Mercedes choked on a laugh. "I'll go with you. Who knows, maybe I'll come up with some fodder for the blog." Then she got a faraway look in her eyes. "You know, I should really talk to her, I bet she can give me some great material."

"Don't even think about it, Mercy."

"Alright," she agreed, but the faraway look never left her eyes.

THERE WAS SOMETHING ABOUT Times Square that appealed to Jeff. The lights, the gaudiness—it was commercialization gone wild. When he was a kid, Times Square had been a different sort of place, a little seedy, a little trashy, but he'd watched the transformation take place. A butterfly coming out of its cocoon. Some days he'd take the subway to Times Square just to be in the presence of all that energy.

Today, people were wall-to-wall, a combination of the Wednesday business lunch crowd and the summer tourists, along with some street preachers and the Naked Cowboy, and he thought he spotted a guy walking a llama.

Just another day in the city. And on any given day, a union strike was happening. Doormen, sanitation workers, electricians, babysitters, bartenders and Broadway musicians. Today, in the heart of Times Square, the electricians were up at bat.

The picket signs were out, men in blue-collar clothes fighting for fair wages, and naturally, the giant blow-up rat that looked as if it came out of a Tim Burton movie. No strike was complete without the rat.

He and Mercedes stood outside the ESPN Sports-Zone restaurant, waiting for Sheldon.

And waiting.

And waiting.

She was late.

Jeff checked his watch and was considering calling her on his cell when he spied the blond hair blowing in the summer wind. Heads turned as she walked by, they always did, wondering who she was. Some people knew and whispered. Those were the ones who followed the tabloids.

Yeah, Sheldon drew eyes. She always drew Jeff's eyes. He didn't understand her, but he liked to look at her, that was for sure.

There was an energy about Sheldon, an electricity, and no matter how empty and unthinking she appeared, she couldn't hide the energy. Sometimes, like now, she let it shine, and when she did, even Times Square looked dim.

She saw him and waved, and half of the picket line waved back.

"That's her, right?" asked Mercedes, poking him in the ribs.

"Yeah."

"Why's she wearing a suit?"

Hallelujah, Sheldon was wearing a demure blue blazer and matching skirt. Yeah, the skirt was kinda short, but he'd take his victories where he could.

"Because she's finally starting to listen to me," answered Jeff.

"Sorry I'm late," Sheldon said, coming up through the crowd, flushed and out of breath. She looked at Mercedes. "I know you, don't I? I really suck at names. I'm Sheldon."

"Mercedes Brooks."

"Ahh…" she said, and she looked at Jeff, wheels spinning behind expressionless blue eyes. "This is your sister? *The Red Choo Diaries?*"

"You know?" said Mercedes.

"Hell, yes. I never miss it."

And *that* was a disaster waiting to strike. Jeff took Sheldon by the arm, away from Mercedes's sly maneuverings before his sister could damage Sheldon's reputation even more. "Right. Sheldon, let's go over to the picket line. I've talked to the union boss, and there's some press lined up, too. I wrote a few lines for you. You don't have to say much. Pick up the picket sign, walk with the workers, maybe do some chanting. Smile and wave. Look pretty. That's pretty much it. Can you handle this?" Jeff handed her the piece of paper with his notes.

She looked over the paper, looked back up at him, blinking fair, soft-looking lashes. "Smile, wave, look pretty? Sure. Not a problem."

There was something different about her today. *Too* eager, *too* cooperative, *too* peppy. Sheldon was never peppy. Jeff tried to ignore the pit in his stomach that said something was wrong with this picture. He watched her walk toward the line, brisk, businesslike and completely confident.

Yeah, something was definitely wrong.

Cameras started to flash, and she raised a hand and waved to everyone. Tourists stopped in the middle of Times Square, trying to figure out which movie star she was.

Mercedes walked over to where Jeff was standing. "You know, I didn't give her enough credit. She's definitely working this, isn't she?"

Sure enough, Sheldon was shaking hands with the workers, talking to one reporter, and in general, dazzling them all.

The pit in his stomach grew two sizes, and Jeff made his way through the strikers. Just as he arrived at the front lines, Sheldon held up a hand and the buzz of the crowd quieted.

"When I read about the electricians' union going on strike, I got mad. This city depends on the electricians to keep Times Square lit up, to keep businesses and hospitals going, in fact, electricians keep people alive. The city depends on electricians to handle the millions of dollars that flow in and out of Wall Street every day."

That was all good, that was all scripted. Jeff began to relax. Then Sheldon turned to the union chief, a grizzled fifty-something with tattooed arms and a blue union cap on his head. "What's your name, sir?"

"Al." he answered, blushing.

She put an arm around the man, drawing him into her world. "We're behind you, Al. The city won't forget about you." She pulled a man who was dressed in a suit from the crowd.

"And what's your name, sir?"

The guy shut off his cell and smiled for the photographers. "Tom."

"Tom, do you support Al here?"

Tom blinked. "Uh, sure."

Sheldon smiled. "So do I. In fact…"

She tugged off her jacket, revealing a lacy black bra beneath. Instantly, the men went wild and a million cameras flashed.

"Oh, this is great stuff for the blog!" Mercedes dove into her purse and produced a digital camera.

Sheldon reached around her back and Jeff closed his eyes.

He knew. He just knew.

A huge cheer went up and Jeff opened his eyes.

There was Sheldon, surrounded by two thousand members of New York City's electricians union, holding the bra triumphantly above her head. Jeff knew their thoughts exactly as they goggled at the golden skin that would never need airbrushing, and the two perfect breasts. Breasts that made his mouth water.

And because of the press he had supplied, invited actually, it was a picture that most of the world would see in tomorrow's papers.

Sheldon grinned, threw her bra in the direction of the photographers and posed. Then, with a satisfied smile, she put back on the demure blue jacket and walked over to Jeff, confident, brisk. Once again, all business.

She grinned at him. "You know, I gotta say, this was a super-great idea. Score one for the 'little man,' right?"

4

SHELDON WALKED TWO BLOCKS before Jeff spoke to her. Even then he didn't say anything to her, just pointed toward a coffee shop, like an owner disciplining a pet.

Oh, he was furious. Steaming. She could see the heat rolling off him. She should laugh, but that would be petty, so she stayed with the ever-popular vacant and guileless expressions.

Once they were inside the café, he sat her down abruptly. "Don't move," he ordered.

Obediently, she sat, her face resting on one hand, watching as he went to the counter. The T-shirt was wonderfully fitted. Knowing Jeff, he had planned it that way, and the jeans—oh, mama. Sheldon didn't usually find herself leering at a man's body, she'd always considered herself a face girl, but Jeff's body was so pleasing to the eye, she could study him for days—and nights. She wasn't nearly done ogling him when he returned with two lattes.

"That was dirty, underhanded and completely over the top," he started out.

"You didn't like it?" she asked, blinking twice.

"Don't play that game with me, Sheldon. I know you."

She gave him a slow smile. "Yes, yes, you do. I think the mayor was there. Did you see him in the back?"

"The mayor?" Jeff buried his face in his hands. "My career is shot to hell. Your father is going to fire me."

She slapped him on the arm. "No, he won't. The company's stock has already shot up two points, and I think I saw a CNN crew in the crowd."

He raised his head, and there was something new in his eyes that made her tingle all over. Respect. Sheldon saw it so rarely, she almost didn't recognize it. His mouth pulled into a rueful smile, and she got more tingles. This time, the carnal kind.

"You know, when you're upset, why don't you say something?"

"I don't get upset, Jeff. I get even."

He shook his head and began to laugh.

"So you were surprised?" she asked.

"Not really."

She put a hand on his bare arm, not necessarily to stroke his forearm, but, well, accidents happen. "Come on, admit it. You were surprised."

"I was not."

"Not even a little?" she asked, leaning forward, letting her jacket gape open. His eyes drifted down. Sheldon felt a flush that had nothing to do with the summer heat.

Under her fingers, she felt the tension in him, and she wished he would let go. "Put it away, Sheldon."

She removed her arm, closed her jacket and crossed her arms across her chest. "Fine. What happened to your sister?"

"She went off to write. Inspiration like you doesn't happen to her very often."

Sheldon couldn't keep her lips from curving up. "What can I say?"

He glared so quickly she changed the subject. "So, what's next on the five-point plan?"

The glare in his eyes softened, and for a minute she felt that tug inside her. "You really hate that, don't you, Sheldon?" he asked, his voice lingering on her name.

"No, what made you think that?"

His look said he knew the answer, but he didn't call her on it. "Fine, let's move on. The next one is easy. We go to a Mets game on Saturday afternoon."

"You'll come with me, then?" she asked, mulling the possibilities.

"You think I'd let you go by yourself?"

"Well, no, but I would like having you there." It was the truth. Jeff was the first man to see through her. Most men couldn't get past her veneer, but Jeff had veneers of his own.

"You'll behave?"

She blinked. "Certainly. I'm a team player."

THE NEXT MORNING, WHEN JEFF arrived at work, he knew there'd be hell to pay. Although he wasn't prepared for it that early.

Phil greeted him with a jaunty wave. "Wayne Summerville will be here in ten minutes. I took the liberty of assembling the press clippings from your daytime excursion yesterday. *USA Today. New York Times*—I like what they did with the pixilation, very natural looking— and here's a press release from the AFL-CIO. They were very happy with the publicity." He took out another sheet of paper. "And the International Brotherhood of

Electrical Workers, Local 47, wants to give Ms. Summerville a plaque for her efforts to advance their cause."

Jeff glanced at the clippings and noticed one piece absent. "Was there anything in *The Red Choo Diaries?*"

"I didn't see that in Google," answered Phil, as he typed in some keys, and then brought up Mercedes' Web site on his computer. "It's a story on… oh, my," he said, leaning into the screen. Finally, he looked up. "It's not Miss Summerville unless she suddenly took a job as an intern at a brokerage house."

"I can't believe she didn't print the pictures," muttered Jeff. Mercedes? His sister? Actually practicing restraint? He'd have to thank her for that.

"Do you want me to print this story about the intern, sir? I should tell you that corporate policy forbids the use of the company computers for nefarious means. Page forty-three in the manual. Would you like to read it?"

Mercedes' good deed notwithstanding, the articles about Sheldon were enough to cause a man serious pain. Jeff took a deep breath. "No, thank you, Phil. I'm going into my office now. Can you bring me some aspirin?"

In less than two minutes, Phil was in Jeff's office, plopping two pills on the desk, along with a glass of water. "Extra-strength." Then he propped himself on the corner of Jeff's desk. "I really like that shirt. Where'd you get it?"

Jeff took the pills and downed them with water. "So you can go out and buy one just like it?"

"I was merely asking. Don't get snippy."

"I'm not snippy," snapped Jeff.

Phil got up in a huff.

"Snippy," he said, and then shut Jeff's door behind him.

EIGHT MINUTES LATER—Jeff was counting—Wayne Summerville arrived, his beefy face flushed from the heat. "Morning, boy," he said, settling himself in the chair opposite Jeff. "I suppose you've seen the papers."

Jeff swallowed. "Yes."

"Then I suppose you know why I'm here."

"I can guess. However, I saw where Summerville Consumer Products stock rose two percent yesterday."

Wayne didn't look happy. "So, what are we going to do about this problem, Jeff?"

"We're moving on to step two now. I've got tickets to the Mets game on Saturday afternoon. It'll be good."

Wayne steepled his fingers. "And do you think my daughter will be able to keep her clothes on for baseball?"

Jeff met Wayne's gaze evenly. "I've been meaning to ask you something, sir. Are you sure that Sheldon's all right with this marriage? Have you thought that this might not be what she wants?"

"Sure, this is what she wants. There's only one thing that drives Sheldon, and that's Sheldon."

"Well, yes, that's probably true, but have you asked her?"

Wayne leaned forward, his eyes narrowing. "I'm not a stupid man, Mr. Brooks. I may be from the country, but I know people. I've asked Sheldon lots of times if she's okay with this. I explained to her the advantages, the disadvantages and the realities of the situation. And time and time again, do you know what she's told me?"

"What?"

Wayne drilled his finger on the desk. "That this is what she wants. I love my daughter, Mr. Brooks, and if

I thought she wasn't one hundred percent on board, I wouldn't go through with it."

"And she's one hundred percent on board with it?"

"Has she told you otherwise?"

"No." Jeff paused, then tried again. "Have you talked to Sheldon about her behavior yourself, sir? She might listen to her father."

Wayne's face twisted into a pained grimace best suited for an antacid commercial. "We don't communicate much. I love my daughter, truly, but sometimes I think she's off on another planet."

"I'm not sure I can get through to her either."

Wayne leaned forward. "But you gotta try, boy. I know you media types. Y'all can sell air conditioners to Eskimos, so I figure you can sell Sheldon on your ideas, too. I think she listens to you."

"Why do you say that?"

"A man's got to believe in something."

"Oh," sighed Jeff, wishing that there was some tangible evidence that Sheldon was coming around.

"Well, good, then we're all in agreement. Now, let's talk about this plan of yours. Since we can safely say that step one was shot to hell in a great big ball of smoke, let's up the ante a bit." Wayne pulled out his checkbook and began to write. "See here, this is a check made out to Jeff Brooks. Check out all those zeros, Jeff." He waved the check under Jeff's nose. "In my world, money talks. And this money is saying, 'boy, you should hope that Sheldon behaves, the Mets win and that my wife stays happy.'" Then he took the check and put it back in his shirt pocket. "I give you my word, that check is yours if Saturday goes through like a greased cat in the dairy."

Jeff nodded in an appropriately deferring manner. "Of course, sir. That's a nice offer, but you don't have to do it."

Wayne got up and slapped Jeff on the arm. "I do, too, boy. This is New York, ain't it? If I can't buy off people here, gosh darn, my money ain't worth a plug nickel."

He went to the door and pointed in Jeff's direction. "Saturday. I'm betting on you, Jeff."

WHILE THE SUMMERVILLE FAMILY headed to Southampton, Sheldon elected to leave later, telling everyone she was shopping. Instead of hitting the LIE with her driver, she did what she did every Friday, and popped in at an apartment building on Central Park West. She didn't like to be recognized, so she wore a short black wig for her visits.

Central Park West was a discreet building where people lived when they didn't want to be noticed. It catered to the likes of movie stars, singers, old New York money and world-famous musicians.

When she knocked on the door at 23C, the others were already assembled in the tastefully decorated room. There was Ling, who was fourteen, Emily who was in her junior year at NYU, Caroline, who was a housewife from the suburbs, and then there was Sheldon, who used the alias Sarah.

They were all there for one purpose: to practice chamber music with the great instructor Stefan Senarsky. For six years Sheldon had been taking private violin lessons from Stefan, but playing solo limited her music choices, so last year she had switched to the chamber class. Now, she wouldn't trade her group for the world.

Music suited her, it soothed her. She loved the

solitude and the tranquility that came from the melody, notes that echoed inside her when she played. Some people believed in yoga, Sheldon believed in music. It didn't care if you were rich, it wouldn't hit up for a loan for another "worthwhile cause," it didn't care who you friends were or weren't. Music simply was.

Stefan, was a conductor in the old-world tradition. He ruled with an iron fist and demanded the best of his students. Actually, Sheldon suspected he was a cupcake inside, but she never told him that. He was going on seventy now, with a long gray beard and silver glasses that couldn't hide the passion in his eyes as he listened to the music.

"Sarah, you're late," barked Stefan.

"Sorry, sir," Sheldon said, and pulled her violin case from the Saks shopping bag, where she kept it hidden. Next, she removed her violin and hurried over to sit in her chair next to Emily. Then Sheldon raised the bow, and joined in a rousing rendition of Schubert's String Quartet in D Minor.

For a few minutes she was lost in the sound, lost in the back and forth of the melody. Schubert wasn't her favorite, but it really didn't matter. Sheldon simply loved to play.

At the end of the piece, Stefan tapped his conductor's baton on the music stand. "Sarah, you were flat on the second stanza. You haven't been practicing. We will begin again."

Truthfully, she had practiced a few hours, but re-styling one's image took time out from a busy socialite's day, so Sheldon had had to cut back some. In fact, she had even delayed seeing Jeff, telling him she would meet him at Central Park after she finished her "shopping."

No one knew about her music, not even Cami. It was the only thing that kept her going. She would never be a professional violinist, never be more than moderately good, but it didn't matter. This was when she was happiest.

Sheldon smiled to herself, pulled her bow back, and began to play.

JEFF LOOKED AT HIS WATCH. Sheldon was late. Again. She'd wanted him to meet her at Chanel. Ha. He'd learned his lesson once, he'd never go shopping with Sheldon again. A man could only suffer so many sleepless nights from watching that much soft, golden, kissable skin.

Deep in his heart, Jeff was a coward. So when he and Sheldon met, they met in "safe" places. Starbucks, Central Park, Chelsea Pier. Places where a man could be tempted to dive in and touch, but he'd get arrested if he did. Whatever worked.

The past few weeks he'd learned a few things about Sheldon. There were depths to her that most people couldn't even comprehend, like her father, for instance. Even Jeff wasn't close to understanding her, but he liked the woman she was so careful to hide. Every once in a while, he saw her there, saw the life flare into her eyes, saw her lips curve up in a smile—a real one, not the smile she gave to the paparazzi.

Jeff understood the value of keeping what was inside you safely hidden. If people didn't know who you really were, they were never disappointed. You were voted Mr. Congeniality or Mr. Goodtime with the Ladies, but never the Man Most Likely to Succeed in Life. For the most part that suited him, but once in a blue moon, the

rare night he was sober and there was no one but
himself, he wondered why he wasn't smarter, why he
wasn't better at business. The streets were packed with
New York success stories. Andrew. Wayne Summerville. Not Jeff. He looked up at the sun, realized there
was no blue moon, and shook off the doubts. Better to
concentrate on the job he was paid to do—fix Sheldon's
image. A job that seemed to be more difficult with every
passing day. However, it would help if the subject in
question was present. Fifteen minutes late. Damn.

While he was waiting, he approached a street vendor
to buy a bottle of water. He'd just reached into his pocket
when he noticed the dark haired woman trotting out
from Central Park West. She was in a modest blue
sundress, and the hair was all wrong, but the walk was
unmistakable.

Jeff put on his sunglasses and watched her go for half
a block. Lo and behold, the dark haired woman pulled off
the wig, exposing her trademark blond locks to the sun.

JEFF WASN'T THERE WHEN SHELDON got to the park, so
she found a bench, put the Saks bag at her feet and
leaned her head back, closing her eyes, letting the sun
stroke her face. She always came from her violin lesson
recharged and revitalized.

Something cold dripped on her face, and suddenly,
there was Jeff. He was wearing sunglasses and a dark
suit that made him look delicious. He always dressed
well, but the tailoring suited him. Coolly sophisticated,
confident, with a smile that could charm even the most
hardened of hearts. Sheldon knew she had a pretty hard
heart, so she could speak from personal experience.

She flashed him a captivating smile of her own.

"Sleeping in the park now?" he asked, sitting down next to her and handing her the bottle of water.

She took a long drink, throat exposed for maximum advantage. "Shopping's hard work," she answered.

"What'd you buy?"

"Another teddy. Want to see?" she teased.

"No," he said in a flat voice, which disappointed her more than it should. "Sorry I'm late. You been here long?"

"No, not long at all. What'd you want?"

"Your father was in my office the other day."

"Surprise, surprise."

"Yeah, well. Sheldon, are you sure this is what you want?"

She curled an arm around his shoulder and leaned in close, close enough to smell his designer cologne, close enough to smell the soap that he used and close enough to smell him. That tantalizing aroma seduced her every time he was nearby. "Of course. Why don't we go back to your apartment, Jeff? Spend the afternoon in bed."

He slid away from her. "Where've you been, Sheldon? I know you weren't shopping." He took off his sunglasses, and she got a good look at the dark, dreamy brown eyes. Eyes that currently weren't so dreamy. Jeff was not happy.

Again.

"What do you think I was doing? I had music lessons, Jeff."

"What's his name?"

And voilà, he had given her the perfect out. "Stefan. He's European," she said in a voice that implied satisfaction had been achieved by all.

"You're almost engaged."

"Almost," she reminded him.

"Will that change anything?"

It was a question she'd thought about for a long time. If she had been in love with Joshua Conrad of Con-Mason U.S.A., the answer would be yes. But she wasn't.

"Nope," she replied, and his mouth tightened into one firm line.

"You had your shot, Jeff, and I have needs," she told him, pulling out a tube of lipgloss and applying it to her pouted lips.

"Fine," he answered. "I bought you a Mets jersey for the game. Wear it. It'll look good for the photo op."

He stood, tossed the shirt in her lap and walked away. After he left, Sheldon sat there alone for a few minutes.

She probably shouldn't have egged him on, but he'd had a chance to believe the truth, and he hadn't.

Sheldon was surprised at how much that hurt.

5

SHEA STADIUM DIDN'T have the history of Yankee Stadium and wasn't as big. It was located in Queens, directly in the flight path of LaGuardia International Airport. All in all, Shea was the bastard son of the New York City ballparks; however, the Mets had changed all that.

They had started to win.

Sheldon liked the Yankees. They had flash, cash and knew how to hit. However, Jeff had stubbornly insisted on the Mets, so, Hello, Shea Stadium.

It was the first time in five years that a Summerville had set foot in Queens.

Thankfully, their seats were in the VIP section, right behind the Mets dugout. If there was a VIP in the name, it couldn't be all bad.

"Hot dog?" asked Jeff.

Sheldon pushed down her sunglasses and stared. "I don't think so."

He lifted his beer. "Just asking. So, how much do you know about baseball? I can give you some details if you'd like—so you don't get bored."

Sheldon pondered that for a second. She knew the Washington Nationals were overrated, thought the National League had it right by not allowing the designated hitter and believed the Yankees had paid too much money for Randy Johnson. "I don't know much," she answered. "Why don't you fill me in?"

And so he proceeded to go into an in-depth tutorial on the rules of baseball and the history of the institution.

Jeff had just finished explaining how the curse of the Chicago Cubs had allowed the 1969 Mets to pull out the National League pennant and go on to win the World Series, when Sheldon interrupted. "You really like this game, don't you?"

He pulled a glove from under his seat. "Nineteen eighty-five New York Metro Division Little League champs, autographed by Mookie Wilson."

Then he grinned the smile of every second-grade boy who'd hit his first home run.

Inside her heart the ice began to melt, a quick, snapping of frozen matter that wasn't fun. It hurt like hell. Sheldon wanted to be tough, she needed to be tough, but when Jeff smiled like that, like pots of gold hung out at the end of rainbows, lotteries were made to be won, and the Mets could take the pennant from the Braves....

Hell. She couldn't stop herself from slipping deeper and deeper into the fathomless water.

All these raw feelings for a man who refused to touch her.

She pulled at the brim of the baseball cap. "Well, well. You know, I changed my mind. I think I want that hot dog after all."

"With mustard?" he asked, and she knew this was important, just by the gravity in his voice.

"And relish, too. Please."

IN THE MIDDLE OF THE SEVENTH, with two outs, Beltran hit a ground-skipping single out to left field, and the lead runner made it to second.

It was the second-best highlight of the game. The first was when Sheldon stole his cap and then jammed it on her head. He stole it back, but it wasn't the same cap anymore. Every time he moved his head he got a momentary whiff of her shampoo, what summer would smell like if they could put it in a bottle.

Sometimes—a lot of the time if he were honest, which he usually wasn't—he'd find her occupying his thoughts, and not all the time was nudity involved. Although, if it was late at night, and always when he was in the shower, nudity *was* involved.

But when he was at work, trying to write out a press release or when he was on the phone to some client, she'd pop into his head.

Jeff frowned.

Sheldon touched his arm. "Something wrong?"

"Nah. Shirt looks good on you," he said.

And it did. It was too big to be sexy, but it worked. The dark blue made her eyes look soft, and her hair ran loose down the back. Mainly she looked relaxed. Not my-pulse-never-beats-over-60 relaxed, but really, truly relaxed. She seemed to be having a good time, and when she had smeared relish on her hot dog, he was pretty sure the press had gotten a picture of it. Now that was award-winning PR.

The crowd started coming alive, and Jeff looked up to see the runner stealing third, with the new Mets rookie sensation, Cal Cooper, still up at bat. The stadium began to chant, starting low, then gaining volume.

"Who's that?" asked Sheldon.

"Cal Cooper. He's hitting .322 so far this year."

"So, this is good?" she asked.

"Oh, yeah."

The first pitch was high and outside. Cooper held firm. Second pitch was a fast ball, Cooper swung and missed.

He took one more swing at a breaking ball, and it flew up,

up,

up,

…past the left foul line.

Shit.

"One and two," she said, her fingernails digging into his thigh. "He hasn't been much of a clutch hitter this season."

Jeff glanced her way, appraising.

She shrugged and went back to watching the game.

The pitch came, a high, hanging slider that seemed to sit in mid-air forever. Cooper pulled back, and

Boom!

The stadium roared.

That ball was gone.

Sheldon jumped up and hugged him, and when she went to plant a kiss on his cheek, *oops,* it seemed the right thing to turn his head, because he needed to taste her.

She froze, and then her arms crept around his neck, and while fifty-seven-thousand Mets fans whistled and cheered and stamped their feet, Jeff Brooks kissed Sheldon Summerville like she was the only woman alive. In that instant, hidden in the crowd, he could forget she was about to be engaged. He could forget about a continental prick named Stefan. Right now, with her willing lips tasting like baseball, relish and lip gloss, he just needed to kiss her.

Just once.

His heart pounded, and he realized that was Sheldon pounding on his chest.

"We need to sit down," she whispered.

The fog cleared from his eyes, and it dawned on him that the crowd was all seated.

Amid a smattering of applause from their section, Jeff and Sheldon sank down in their seats. Jeff jammed on his sunglasses and pulled his hat low.

"Do you think anybody noticed?" he asked, eyeing the press box upstairs.

Sheldon stared at the Diamond-Vision JumboTron. Playing on the forty-six-foot screen was a slow-motion video replay of Sheldon in Jeff's arms.

"I don't think anyone noticed at all," she answered, putting on her sunglasses.

They didn't touch each other for the rest of the game, and the Mets won seven to four.

SUNDAY MORNING WAS A LAZY time for Sheldon. Her apartment wasn't modern but comfortable, with a Persian rug on the floor and tons of pillows. Her habit was to sleep late, then spread the Sunday paper on the rug, sipping her coffee.

This morning she'd had trouble concentrating on the fall fashion forecast, and even her violin practice wasn't cutting it. Her mind kept turning to the feel of Jeff's mouth on her own. And when her mind wasn't accurate enough, she could replay the video clip she'd found on the *Sports Illustrated* Web site. The site wondered about the identity of the lucky man, but Sheldon knew there were just as many women who wanted to be held that tightly, with such desperation.

God, the man had a marvelous technique. All passion and verve.

No, Sheldon was the lucky one in that equation, and because she wanted to feel lucky again, she watched the clip and sighed. She was halfway through her sixteenth viewing when her mother arrived.

Cynthia was dressed in a linen shirt and white capris, with gold, dangling earrings that dangled below her perfectly styled hair. Sheldon was still dressed in a blue undershirt.

That earned a look.

"How's it going, Mom? Want some coffee, I'll pour you a cup."

Cynthia moved aside the papers on the table and sat, her face all business. Sheldon steeled herself for the lecture to come.

"This has got to stop, Sheldon."

"What?" asked Sheldon, picking up a pillow from the couch and cradling it against her chest.

"Who was with you at the baseball game yesterday?"

"No one," answered Sheldon.

"Stop it."

Sheldon studied her mom. She loved her, and in ordinary circumstances she could have gushed on and on about Jeff. All about his plan to "fix" her, all about the tingles under her skin when he looked at her. However, these weren't ordinary circumstances. Sheldon was engaged. Almost.

"He's European. His name is Stefan. He comes to New York sometimes. It's nothing, Mom."

"You're embarrassing Josh."

Sheldon threw the pillow onto the couch. "Josh doesn't care. Besides, he probably sleeps with eighteen different women every week. You're the only one who cares."

"Your father was furious."

"Really?" asked Sheldon, wishing she were there to see that. It took a lot to make her dad mad.

"He was ready to fire the PR firm that's working with you."

"He can't do that."

"Why not?"

Sheldon thought hard. "Contracts."

"If they're not doing their job, there's no reason for your father to pay them, is there?" asked her mother, who had a valid point. A point that Sheldon had overlooked.

Quickly, she spoke to rectify that mistake. "It's me, not them. I'll behave, Mom. I'll be the soul of discretion. The angel you've always wanted."

"You're the daughter I've always wanted, Sheldon. I worry about you," said Cynthia, taking a sip of Sheldon's coffee, leaving a red line of lipstick on the cup.

"Sure."

"Seriously. Cami always knew exactly what she wanted, and she went for it. You were always quiet. Kept to yourself. I never knew what you were thinking. You didn't argue, didn't express an opinion."

"I have opinions."

"Don't keep them to yourself, honey."

"Sure, Mom."

"And another thing…"

"Yes?"

"Where's Cami?"

Uh-oh. "What do you mean?"

"I thought you and her were going to do something together. She said she was spending the weekend with you. She's not with Lance, is she?"

"You've met him?" asked Sheldon curiously. She hadn't even met him yet.

"No! But I've heard enough. He's a musician," uttered her mother as if that made him a criminal.

"She's studying. I had asked her to cover for me. You know, because of Stefan. I didn't want you know," she answered, hanging her head in a marvelous imitation of shame.

Her mother's perfectly shaped eyebrows pulled together, and she lowered her voice to a whisper. "Stefan…he's not here, is he?"

"No, Mom. He had to fly back to Italy last night."

"He's Italian?"

"Oh, yeah. Dark, handsome. I love to hear him talk."

"I always wanted an Italian lover."

"You?"

"Oh, yes. Your father is wonderful, but he's not, 'exotic,' you know?"

"Mom, you're a devil."

In a rare moment, mother and daughter shared a look of understanding. Sheldon had never thought of her mom in that way before, and it made her feel better. Less like some genetic muck-up.

"You'll behave?"

"Cross my heart," promised Sheldon. And this time, she meant it.

THEA BROOKS WAS AN ASPIRING actress, and whenever she had an acting audition, one member of the Brooks family was elected to run lines with her. It'd been over eighteen months since Andrew and Mercedes had last suckered him into it, and Jeff had ended up portraying a menopausal widow experiencing a second chance at love.

Tonight, it was Mercedes's turn, and both he and Andrew were there to heckle—that is, support—their sister.

Their mother's apartment was a one-story pre-war in Queens with pipes that rattled when the water was turned on and a couch with curved wooden legs that Andrew had carved up when he was working at a furniture factory along the East River. However, all the flaws in the apartment didn't matter. His mom had a special attachment to it, and even though Andrew had offered to buy her a new place, she always declined. "This one is my lucky apartment. If I move, I'll never get a part."

Since she'd only had two parts in her life, and both had come while in residence at said apartment, it was difficult to argue with that logic.

As soon as he got in the door, Mercedes held up the picture from the sports section of *Newsday: Sheldon And Mystery Lover.*

She stabbed at the paper with her index finger. "That's you."

"No, I wasn't there," answered Jeff calmly, placing the bags of Chinese food on the table. Plausible deniability. "I had a date," he said. "Very hot," he added, because they'd expect him to say that.

Andrew sat on the carved-up couch. One leg casually crossed over the over. "She's your client, and that's your scar."

"What scar?" asked Jeff, still sticking firmly to plausible deniability.

His mother piped in. "On the side of your neck. The one you got from jumping off the fire escape when you were eight. Scared me to death, all that blood. We spent the night at the E.R. in St. Joseph's."

"I don't have a scar," said Jeff, his palm covering his neck.

Andrew coughed. "I gotta say, Jeff, you are doing one bang-up job of fixing her reputation. She's flashing the union guys, making out with her PR flunkie in the middle of eighty thousand Mets fans—"

"—and don't forget the national television audience. I saw it on the eleven o'clock news," added Mercedes. "Now that's some good exposure."

"Nobody knows it's me," muttered Jeff, sorting through the kung pao chicken and steamed dumplings.

"How much will you pay us to keep quiet? I've got rent due in two weeks. The cash would come in handy."

Andrew looked at Mercedes. "You aren't making enough to pay your rent?"

Jeff threw a paper napkin at Andrew, then asked, "Where's Jamie?"

"She had to work."

"Slave driver."

"She's not that comfortable with family gatherings," Andrew finally admitted. "Yet. You guys really scare her."

"You've been thinking, haven't you?" prodded Jeff, mainly to see his brother sweat.

"Thinking about what?" asked their mother, sitting down to eat.

"He's going to ask Jamie to marry him," explained Mercedes, not bothering to sit. She stood, noshing on rice.

"I didn't say that," said Andrew.

"He's chicken. Scared shitless by the idea of long-term commitment to one woman."

"That's not Andrew, that's you, Jeff," said Mercedes.

"Thank you," said Andrew.

"I like Jamie," their mother said. "You should propose. Good women don't grow on trees."

"I'll do this on my own time," insisted Andrew, picking up his plate and returning to sit alone on the couch.

"He's chicken," said Jeff, loudly enough for Andrew to hear.

"The decision of who to spend the rest of your life with, who to have children with, who to buy a house with, shouldn't be made too quickly."

"Oh, come on." Jeff knew when he was on to a good thing. "You know Jamie's the one. You just don't like all the crap that comes with a wedding. Picking out china, bridal showers—"

"You know, they have couple's showers now," interrupted Mercedes.

"I went to one for Lillian Stewart's oldest daughter a few months ago. It was very nice," said Thea.

"I'm not getting married," snapped Andrew.

"We won't tell Jamie that," said Jeff.

Andrew looked at his brother, his eyes sneaky. "You're one to talk, Jeff. When are you gonna get married? Honestly, when's the last time you went on a date?"

"Yesterday," said Jeff quickly.

"I thought Sheldon was a client?" asked Mercedes.

"She is," Jeff agreed, concentrating on his rice.

"So it wasn't a date?" asked Andrew.

"No," said Jeff, still concentrating on the rice. Heavily concentrating. Food was much easier to fathom than Sheldon.

"It wasn't a date, and you kissed her—" Andrew pointed at the paper "—like *that?*"

"Yes," replied Jeff, feeling the walls close in around him.

Andrew smiled. It was the smile that kicked Jeff in the gut. "It wasn't a date," he muttered to himself.

Mercedes high-fived Andrew. "Nice job, bro." Then she looked at Jeff. "You know, Wedgwood makes the nicest china. For the silver, consider Oneida."

6

FOR THE ENTIRE weekend, Jeff had kept his cell turned off, fearing the messages from Wayne Summerville. His best estimate was that there would be five messages on the cell and two waiting at the office. Less than that wasn't believable, any more than that, Jeff didn't want to contemplate.

Eventually, Monday morning rolled around, and Jeff couldn't dodge the consequences any longer.

He arrived promptly at nine and looked at Phil calmly. "Any messages?" he asked

"Seventeen," answered Phil. "'Wayne Summerville—Call me,' 'Wayne Summerville—Why haven't you called me?' 'Wayne Summerville—I pay you good money, you better gosh-darn return my calls,' 'Wayne Summerville—'"

Jeff held up a hand, all pretenses of calm fading rapidly. "I get the idea."

"Ms. Summerville is making it difficult for you, sir?"

"More than you could comprehend. I thought I knew how to handle women, but every time I think I've got her figured out, she takes off some piece of clothing, and I end up standing there wiping the drool from the side of my mouth. Damnedest thing."

"Have you tried being nice to her, Mr. Brooks?"

"Don't get snippy, Phil."

Phil held up innocent hands. "Simply saying that sometimes you can be something of a bear."

Jeff scowled. "I'm nothing like a bear. I'm easygoing, relaxed, fun-loving and people like being around me."

"I'm only saying," repeated Phil, handing over seventeen pink message slips.

Jeff shook his head sadly. "Do you have some aspirin?"

"Right here, Mr. Brooks. Also, I added a little twist of lemon."

Jeff popped the pills into his mouth and took a long swallow. "You're a peach, Phil. Send in Mr. Summerville when he gets here."

Phil perked right up. "Whatever you say, boss."

WAYNE SUMMERVILLE SHOWED UP at ten. At 10:01 a.m., the yelling commenced.

"I gave you fair warning, Mr. Brooks!"

Jeff pointed to the legal pad that he'd used for his notes. "I'm sorry, sir. I've written down some potential options for our five-point plan. I know you're disappointed."

"Disappointed? That my daughter is making moonshine with some Eye-talian Stallion whose name I can't even pronounce?"

Jeff stopped pointing and put down his pen. "What?"

"Do I have to repeat myself? I said I couldn't pronounce it."

"She said the man was an Italian?" asked Jeff.

"I don't care what the son of a bitch's name is, because the important thing to remember is that it's not Josh, her fiancé."

"Not yet, sir," reminded Jeff. Semantics were important. So Sheldon had lied to her father about whom she was kissing? Fascinating. However, as fascinating as that was, right now he needed to focus on keeping the client happy.

Considering the red shade of Wayne Summerville's nose, Wayne was several emotions removed from happy. The man leaned down, his eyes conveying many things, and none of them would be described as happy.

"I'm giving you and the kindly folks at Columbia-Starr one last chance, and then I'll have no choice but to take my business elsewhere."

"Yes, sir," said Jeff, pasting a confident smile on his face.

"And by the way," Wayne continued, completely ignoring Jeff's efforts at diffusing the anger in the situation, "I have something for you." He pulled out a piece of paper and began unfolding it before Jeff's eyes. "You remember this?" he asked, pointing to the check that still contained Jeff's name.

"Yeah."

Wayne began ripping the check into tiny pieces. When he was done, he scattered them over Jeff's desk. "Are we clear, Mr. Brooks."

Jeff was still smiling. "Crystal."

ON TUESDAY, JEFF MET SHELDON at the Museum of Modern Art. He wasn't a huge fan of the museum, believing that nude pictures of women should be pleasing to the eye, not put together like a jigsaw puzzle. However, he was there today because he was determined to keep Sheldon on a short leash, and he thought if she decided to get naked—always a distinct possibility—people might mistake it for modern art.

They sat down in front of a Dali painting. "We're down to one last shot, Sheldon."

"One last shot to fix my image?" she said, blinking innocently.

He smiled patiently. "No, one last shot before Columbia-Starr is fired."

"Oh," she answered, this time with no blinking.

"I really need you to behave this time. No more acting up."

As soon as the words left his mouth, the serene, unexcitable blue eyes lit up like a neon billboard. Man, he loved to push her buttons. Even better, she began poking him in the chest. "I was on my best behavior. I was an angel at that baseball game before you—you—mauled me."

Jeff's bubble of momentary happiness faded. "Mauled you? Hello? Was that *your* tongue in my mouth?"

The patrons around them began to stare, a nearby teacher hurried her young students away. Sheldon, finally learning the art of being discreet, lowered her voice. "You were lucky, Jeff. You know most men would jump at the chance to have my tongue in their mouth."

Sadly, she was correct, but he wasn't about to admit it. Honestly, the idea just pissed him off even more. Jeff rolled his eyes. "Wow, Miss 'the World Wants to Sleep with Me and Maybe I'll let them.' I get my share of attention from the opposite sex, too, you know. Women are always throwing themselves at me. Always," he said, crossing his arms over his chest.

She started to giggle, her eyes holding him captive. "You are such a dog."

The anger inside him died, the tension gone. With a snap of her fingers, his mood jumped from white-hot anger to cock-hardening lust. It wasn't the most comfortable scenario in the world, but Jeff had started to accept it. Sheldon could make him laugh and he got a crazy high whenever she looked at him with her too-blue eyes.

They sat, staring at each other, until finally Sheldon looked away. "Why are we here?" she asked.

Once again, back to reality. Jeff took a deep breath. "You have a dress for Saturday?"

"What's Saturday?"

"The Fourth of July society thing. Some charity. Good cause. Lots of money. Somewhere in the Hamptons. Your dad knows. He didn't tell you?" Jeff asked, upset that Wayne Summerville had left him to do his dirty work.

"No. You'll be there, too?" she asked.

Jeff nodded once. The next part was the hardest. Be a Band-Aid, rip it off. He glanced away before he spoke because he didn't want her to read too much in his eyes.

"So will Josh Conrad. You're supposed to be his date."

THE PARTY WAS AT THE HOME of the illustrious artist, Charlie Something-or-Other. Jeff didn't get the name, but when he walked into the house, he knew that Charlie Something-or-Other must be a really, really, really good artist.

The whole front room was all glass windows, looking out over the ocean, where the sun was beginning to set. Candles flickered everywhere, making the room appear more like the set of a perfume commercial. The furniture was a stark white, and a grand piano took over one corner of the room. Flowers were everywhere, too. In vases, on tabletops, twined on top of the piano. It was interior design on LSD. All in all, the place reeked of class. When Jeff had been growing up, the only time he'd seen places like this was when he'd been cutting the grass or waiting tables. It was hard to think that Andrew could afford a place like this now, but Andrew would have a heart attack and die before he'd spend that much money on such a "worthless piece of real estate that you could never get a good return on."

Jeff laughed to himself. In the end, if something made you happy, did it really matter what sort of rate of return you got?

Nah. He went over to the bar where some blonde in a tuxedo jacket was serving drinks.

"Is this a wine-only bar?" he asked.

She smiled at him, her lips full and glossy. "No, we have lots of things here. What would you like?"

Jeff cleared his throat. "Give me a beer, please. Something domestic if you have it."

"Certainly," she answered, and handed him the beer, her hand lingering. "Will there be anything else?"

Jeff stuffed a five in the tip jar. "Thanks, but no."

He was about to take a sip when he saw Sheldon coming through the doorway. Her whole family had arrived, her father, Mrs. Summerville and her sister. But it was Sheldon who stopped him cold.

Damn.

He'd seen her naked, seen her in her slutty clothes, seen her in blue jeans, but he'd never seen her…like this. Which was totally unfair because he had truly liked her the way she was before, but this woman… This woman was dazzling. A woman a man could never forget. Her dress was long and silver and made of sheer material that flowed around her when she walked. It wasn't cut low or anything, but it certainly didn't hide the curves she had. Jeff wanted to walk up and put an arm around her, just to touch her. But he wouldn't.

Her silvery-blond hair was piled up on her head, loose pieces hanging down, skimming her shoulders. Her skin glowed in the candlelight, and his fingers flexed, once, twice. He moved the beer bottle to the other hand, mainly so he'd have something to hang onto. Goddamn, she made a man want.

Right then, another man came up behind her, put his arm around her, touching her.

He looked like a nice enough guy, young, handsome, rich and completely at home in this sort of place.

Jeff wanted to hit him.

Sheldon caught Jeff's eye. For a minute, she didn't move, and he wondered if she could read his mind, wondered if she could tell how much he longed to touch her, to pull the strap from one shoulder, so he could nuzzle the skin that was there.

Her lips curved in a smile.

Jeff raised his beer in a silent salute.

This was her night, not his.

He was here for only one reason. To make sure everything went perfectly.

SHELDON DID HER BEST TO behave, but her eyes kept straying over to the corner where Jeff was standing alone. He didn't try and mingle, didn't try and make conversation. He simply stood and watched the crowd. Every now and then, their eyes would meet and then slide carefully away.

"Who's the guy in the corner?" asked Cami, coming up to stand next to her sister.

"He works for Dad," said Sheldon.

"I've never noticed him before."

"Yeah, well." She dragged her gaze away from Jeff before Cami noticed anything more. "Hey, I like the Extreme Makeover: Cami Edition. You look good, sis," she said, and Cami did. She was wearing a simple yet sophisticated black cocktail dress with heels. Her sister *never* wore heels.

Cami's gaze shifted left and right, then she whispered, "Lance is coming over here in a while. I had my last exam of the session, so school's out for another six days. I'm living it up while I can."

Sheldon understood that way of thinking. She'd been thinking of living it up while she could, too. "Does Mom know?"

"Has hell frozen? First, he's in a band, second, he has a tattoo, and third, he's not going to college. It's the trifecta of doom. I keep hoping her to come around. It hasn't happened yet."

Sheldon heaved a sigh, being the responsible big sister was a new role for her, and she knew she wasn't up to it. Especially not tonight. "You're going to make me lie, aren't you?"

"Hopefully not. Only if she realizes I've disappeared."

Ah, for the good ole' days when life was simple and the highlight of Cami's life was nothing more exciting than a new bloom on a rose. "Have you seen their gardens yet? Mom said they're awesome."

And suddenly Cami was off to the races. "Are you kidding me? She's got some great roses out there.

Double Delight, and Velvet Abundance, and you should see her English roses."

Right then, Sheldon's glance collided with Jeff's. Again. She'd promised her mother that everything would go smoothly this evening, but there were emotions boiling inside her, feelings that were far from smooth. The old Sheldon would have ran from the room. But this new Sheldon, or at least, she wanted to believe there was a new Sheldon, needed to stand strong and get through this. Her family needed her. Jeff's job depended on her. People expected things from her, and she felt like a nervous wreck. There was no way she was going to get through this night without someone being disappointed in her. It was anybody's guess whether that would be her parents, Jeff, or Josh.

"Come with me," said Sheldon, grabbing Cami's arm, choosing to flee the scene.

Cami shook free. "Can't. I've got to call Lance and give him directions. I told him I'd call as soon as I got here."

"Fine, desert your sister in her time of need," she joked in a shaking voice.

Cami laughed. "Yeah, sure. Listen, you'll cover for me later on, right? You did great the other day."

Sheldon waved her on. "Go, have fun, but don't get arrested, or if you do, don't call me. Dad will blame me."

Cami gave her a quick hug. "You're a great sister."

Sheldon shooed her. "Get outta here before you mess up my make-up. It took me half a day to look this natural."

Then Cami was gone, leaving Sheldon alone. She walked out onto the terrace where the roses were blooming. With the gardens facing the ocean, the patio lit up with candles at sunset, it was a magical place. Sheldon reached out and stroked one of the rose petals, lured by its softness and delicacy. She bent low to smell the beautiful flower, her nose tempted by the aroma.

"Sheldon?"

It was Jeff. Her stomach pulled into knots, and she pretended she didn't hear him, so she could gather her thoughts, keep her eyes vacant and carefree.

His hand touched her bare shoulder, and she jerked upright, but something kept her from moving easily, and it had nothing to do with him.

She was snared by the rosebush.

She pulled once, hard, hearing the fragile fabric give way.

Hell.

Sheldon was free, but parts of her dress were still clinging to the bush. She clutched her hand to the top of her dress, feeling the breeze in places it wasn't supposed to blow.

"What's wrong?" asked Jeff.

"It's torn," said Sheldon, between gritted teeth.

His eyes looked at her suspiciously. She'd been doing her best, she'd told herself she was going to walk this line, and now he didn't believe in her? That hurt.

"Oh, come on, Jeff, I was smelling the roses. Don't you ever just stop and smell the roses? Go get my sister, so I don't have to stand her all night holding my boob."

"I just passed her leaving. She climbed into some car out front."

"She's left? Already?"

"Think so. Yeah." His mouth started to curve. "You look kinda cute like that."

She glared. "All I need is a needle and some thread."

"Won't a safety pin work?"

She looked down at her strap, looked at the delicate material, which the seamstress had spent a day getting to flow exactly right, and shook her head. "Needle and thread."

"Fine. I'll see what I can do. You stand there, smile, look pretty, and try not to flash anybody."

Sheldon stood, slightly bent over, pretending a staggering interest in roses. People gave her curious looks as they passed, and she merely sniffed the flowers and smiled like an idiot. Minutes seemed like hours but, finally, Jeff returned. "Okay, I've got it. We need to find a place to get this fixed up."

"We'll find a bedroom, somewhere private." She glanced around at the crowd milling on the beach and the patio. "You don't you see my parents, do you?"

"No," he said. "But it's not like it's anything they haven't seen before."

"You are such a wise ass, and it is *so* not helping right now."

"Sorry. Some day you'll look back on this and laugh."

With Jeff acting as lead scout, together they found a bedroom off the main hallway. Once inside, Sheldon immediately stripped off her dress.

Jeff froze. "What are you doing?" he asked, and the heat in him was palpable. She felt it. In parts of her she really didn't need to be thinking about at the moment. In the midst of an emergency.

"I'm fixing my dress. Can you help me?"

He shook his head. "Sorry, it always takes me a minute to start thinking again."

She sat on the bed, wearing her panties, hose, and

heels, while Jeff stood helpless. Sheldon tried to thread the needle, but the man was looking at her, and even an idiot could figure out what evil deeds were lurking behind that dark, currently heated gaze.

Sheldon had always considered her body property of the state, a national monument, like the Liberty Bell, or the Empire State Building. It never felt as if it belonged only to her, but to the public. Although when he looked at her, everything became personal.

She could feel the bumps on her skin, her nipples puckered and tightened, a mad pulse throbbing between her legs, and they were so close to a bed, and oh, sweet, merciful bed…

No.

Someone needed to be rational, and it wasn't going to be Jeff. "You're not thinking. Now is not the time for not thinking. I need to get this sewn up before anybody notices I'm gone. I promised Mom that I wouldn't get into any trouble. And you know, she's going to think I'm getting into trouble."

"Hurry it up," he said, all while staring at her chest, which made it impossible to hurry.

"Can you stop looking at me like that?" she asked, and he turned around, but it wasn't any good. She could still feel him—thinking.

"This isn't working," she said.

He tossed her his tux jacket. "Here, wear this while you're that."

She wrapped the jacket around her, and it actually made things worse. It smelled like his cologne, his soap, and best of all, him. That did it—now she wanted him. The lining rubbed against her bare breasts and if she concentrated hard, well, actually not that hard, she could imagine his hands on her breasts.

She pulled the needle through the fabric. Just concentrate, Sheldon.

In, out, in, out, in, out.

Stop it, stop it, stop it, stop it. It took seventeen long, hard strokes of the needle for her to get the strap in some semblance of order. She pulled at the thread with her teeth, yanked, then efficiently tied the knot.

"You do that very well," he said.

"It's a girl thing."

"Whatever," he said.

She stood, stripped off his jacket, and pulled on her dress, not daring to look in his direction. Dear God, she was dying to look in his direction. She was dying to dive in his direction.

But now was not the time.

She opened the door to leave, and Jeff was still standing there.

The man of action stood motionless.

"Well, come on."

He glanced down. "Can't."

And for the first time, she dared look and saw a good eight inches of heaven tenting his pants, just waiting to be explored, and stroked and absorbed inside her.

Sheldon kept staring.

"Can you stop looking at me like that?" he asked. "It only aggravates the situation."

Sheldon knew she couldn't. She didn't want to. She wanted to stop and smell the roses while she still could.

She took a bold step forward, backing him up against the wall, with an authentic Van Gogh painting hanging right behind him. It wasn't exactly what she'd imagined their first time would be like, but she wanted him so badly, and if the gods weren't conspiring for this, then, well, there were no gods.

Her hands slid up his chest, underneath the jacket, and she could feel the line of his pecs. He took a deep breath, his abs rippling under her fingers. It all felt so much better, so much harder, so much more real than her fantasies.

A woman could take a big risk for a man like this.

He didn't touch her, was waiting for her, and she knew he wouldn't. This was all up to her because Jeff had scruples and honor. Sheldon didn't.

Somehow that thought only made things easier. She leaned in close, close enough to smell the cologne and the soap, and pressed a warm, wet kiss to his neck. His skin felt like fire underneath her lips, and she heard him groan.

She reached down, hitting below the belt, and slowly unzipped his fly, feeling his erection spring free from the briefs that tried to contain it.

She stroked the velvety steel, feeling it pulse with each touch. All that power in her hands.

She looked up, finally daring to meet his eyes, and he was watching her, his jaw tight with tension, his gaze heavy-lidded with desire. She took another step closer, letting his cock nuzzle between her thighs.

Just one touch, and she was gonna go off like a rocket.

She took another stroke, because she wanted the power again.

And then from the hallway, she heard a voice calling. "Shel-don?"

All thoughts of rockets firing were cancelled. The

orgasm would have to wait. Later, for instance, when she was alone. "That's my mother."

Sheldon zipped up his pants and planting a quick kiss on his cheek. His eyes were closed, and she suspected he was in severe physical pain. But right now, there were bigger problems to worry about. Well, maybe not bigger, but other problems, definitely.

"Sorry, bud, you're going to have to fly this mission solo," she said, rushing out the door.

After she left the room she was sure that she heard a painful moan.

Sheldon only smiled.

TEN MINUTES LATER, JEFF RETURNED to the party in a state suitable for public consumption. It was just wrong that one woman could render him so stupid and defenseless, all with her body, which she seemed to have no qualms about showing off, to him or to everyone.

He sighed, and spotted the female in question approaching him, mischievous eyes dancing with delight.

"Better?" she asked, lips curving in a smile.

He nodded his head, very much the gentleman, even under moments of great duress. "Much, thank you for asking. Canapé?" he suggested, gesturing to the table laden with food behind her. She snagged a shrimp and two crackers.

Jeff spied an orchid on the table and picked it up. If he was a betting man, which he was, he'd bet that she adored orchids.

Right then, Josh, man of the hour, came up to Sheldon and placed his arm around her as if it belonged there. Forever.

"There you are. Your mom was looking for you."

Her expression dimmed a little, or at least Jeff wanted to think so. "Found me!"

"There's someone I think you should meet…" he was saying.

And so Josh Conrad steered her away, away from Jeff, and on to better things, more suitable things for her life.

Nobody noticed when one crushed orchid fell to the floor. In the big scheme of things, what was one stupid flower going to change, anyway?

7

THE FOURTH OF JULY party was wrapping up, guests leaving, everyone going off to see the fireworks. The full moon was high over the ocean, and in the distance, the popping noises heralded the start of the show.

Sheldon leaned against the terrace wall overlooking the Atlantic. It'd been her first real test, and all things considered it'd gone well. Josh was happy. Her parents were happy. And Jeff, well, she didn't know what he was thinking.

The sea air brushed against her hair, but the normal peace she found by the ocean was gone. Tonight things had been stirred up inside her. Feelings, responsibilities, uncertainties. There was a world out there she was supposed to participate in, but Sheldon wanted to go back into hiding, back on the glass shelf where everything was quiet and peaceful, and no one could hurt her.

She felt him before he spoke. It was that weird mind-thing again. It wasn't a physical feeling, just a shot to her brain that Jeff was there.

"You did good," he said, his hands tucked in his pockets. His black bow tie was loosened and hanging to one side, and the wind had blown though his hair, making it softer, more inviting.

"Thanks."

He stood there next to her, not touching her, and the silence was nice. If only the world would be silent forever.

Sheldon leaned down and pulled off her shoes. "You mind walking down to the beach for a bit? My feet are killing me."

He slung his jacket over his shoulder and nodded, his eyes thoughtful.

"Joshua seems like a nice guy," he said, starting the conversation off with a bang.

"He is." She took a deep breath of sea air. Not even that smell— the one that had always been so comforting to her—lifted her spirits tonight. Such a perfect party. She should feel like Cinderella.

"Don't you ever not want to do this?" he asked, not looking at her, which somehow made it all that much harder to answer.

Sheldon stopped and sat down in the sand, pulling her knees up under her. Jeff sat next to her, but not too close. She'd learned that was his specialty. Never too close.

"Sometimes," she answered, picking up a handful of the coarse sand and letting it slip through her fingers.

"Then why do it? You don't have to."

She braced her arms behind her and leaned back. "The merger is a good deal for my family. Billions of dollars. And there's the employees of Summerville Consumer Products, plus the employees of Con-Mason. Do you know how hard it is to break into the Chinese marketplace? It's pretty well impossible. Do you know what the fastest-growing economy is? China."

"That many Chinese people need white teeth?"

Sheldon smiled. "You know why I'm doing this?

The real reason? I get a chance to do something for my family. I've been a slug my entire life. Cami's going to be a doctor. You know what I'm going to be?"

"What?"

"I don't know either. I should have figured it out by now."

"Maybe that's because you didn't have to."

"Maybe that's because I didn't want to," she answered. It was the truth. The fear that when you set out to discover a lifelong ambition, there would be nothing there.

For a while they sat, lost in the rhythmic sound of the waves, the occasional splash of a fish and the far-off cannons of fireworks.

A flash of green exploded in the sky overhead.

Jeff finally looked at her. "Want a beer?"

"You have one?"

"I have two in my pocket."

"And here I thought you were just glad to see me."

He popped the caps and handed her one. "I do have some talents."

"To worthless ambitions," she said, clinking her bottle to his. "What about you?"

"You want to hear about my worthless ambitions?"

"Yeah," she answered, a red star busting through the dark sky.

"I suppose it doesn't compare to bringing whiter teeth and fresh breath to the fine people of China, but I'm going to buy a boat."

She looked at him, trying to picture him behind the wheel. Yeah, she could see that. "What kind of boat?"

"Something long and sleek with lots of teak and a double-masted sail."

A sailing man. "Very impressive."

"I've got a fund stashed away. Your dad said that after the merger, Columbia-Starr would get all the company's PR business. I figure I'll be able to splurge then."

Sheldon smiled, it something like her father would do. "Dad's good about taking care of people."

"He's all right."

The fireworks boomed overhead with myriad colors. White, green, yellow and blue. She watched the colors dancing around the sky, but even fireworks didn't help her mood. Anxiety. That was the problem.

"Jeff?"

"Yeah?"

"Do you ever think about getting married?"

"Not if I can help it."

"I think of all the things that I have now, and the lack of responsibility. Did you know that marriage is a big responsibility?"

"Yes, ma'am, that I know. The decision of who to spend the rest of your life with, who to have children with, who to buy a house with, all that's huge."

"So you're happy with the way your life is now?"

"It works for me. What about you?"

"Considering the state of the world, it'd be petty and small-minded of me to complain about anything in my life."

"You're allowed to complain about getting married, Sheldon. Hell, I would."

"It's kind of scary. I mean, right now, if I want to do something, anything, I can do it. After I'm married, I have to think."

Suddenly her mind was filled with all the things she

wanted that would be forbidden. Including Jeff. She took a deep drink of her beer, anything to kill the tension between them. The whole night had been one performance after another, and her nerves were basically shot. What was wrong with her? She had the world by the tail, but it all felt like crap. Tonight was a perfect evening, everything running like a clock, yet she was stretched taut, ready to snap. Right now Sheldon just wanted to cry.

"You're not married yet, Sheldon," he said, his voice taut.

"Will you still be my friend?"

"Yeah."

She leaned her head on his shoulder, and he stayed still, but this time she would wait him out.

She didn't have to wait long.

He tilted her chin toward him and kissed her. Lightly, gently.

"You taste like beer," he whispered.

"You taste like Jeff," she answered, and then he kissed her in earnest.

The sound of the water, the feel of his heart and his skin beating against hers was so welcoming. This wasn't pretend, this was real. The salt from the night air made his skin taste like the ocean. The sand underneath her skin, abrading her…

Finally. All the other moments had led up to this, and for Sheldon, it was like a dam breaking inside her. She wanted to come alive, and when he was nearby, she did. He was so careful with his kisses. Not making any promises, but she could taste his need hidden there. Oh, he didn't want to admit it, but she knew it was there, and it only made her want him more.

He pulled her down in the sand and into his arms, his hands twisting in her hair urgently, pulling it down around her shoulders.

"I wanted...to see that," he said, "I wanted to see it...loose." Then he was kissing her again, nipping at her lower lip, and she bit at his, because she wanted him to hurt. Wanted him to feel on the level that he made her feel.

Jeff pulled at the straps of her dress, and she felt the mended one give, but she didn't care. There was no one left to see but him, and he'd already seen far more private parts of her than anyone else ever knew existed.

He lowered her dress, his hands on her breasts and in the moonlight, she could see his face so clearly, his eyes sharp with desire, his mouth tight, every muscle in his body pulled to breaking. Here was Mr. Smooth Operator brought low by lust.

For her.

She put her hands underneath his shirt, feeling the warm, hard flesh, feeling the sweat on his skin, feeling the pound of his blood underneath. Frantically she pulled at the studs on his shirt, but gave up and ripped them free, until his chest was open for her to explore. Roughly he put a knee between her legs and she settled herself against it, riding his thigh like it was him, and Sheldon felt a moan rise deep in her throat. This was what she wanted, this was what her body craved. Already she was so wet, so ready.

He lowered his head, his mouth against her breast, and she felt the rasp of his stubble against her skin. It should have burned. It felt like heaven. He pulled at the taut nipple, his mouth suckling there, teeth and tongue working in rhythmic concert. Despite the heat in the air, Sheldon began to shake.

A woman could die from this.

He looked up, stared at her. She tried to breathe, but it was so much.

"Are you all right?" he asked.

She nodded once.

"Good," he said, and then his hand was between her thighs, pushing her panties aside. "Sheldon, I didn't want to do this. I tried. I really tried." Then his finger shoved inside her and flicked against her clit. Sheldon stopped maintaining any semblance of reason. Needing something to hold on to, all she could find was sand.

Now, she thought.

Now, she thought, her fingers fumbling at his fly. She needed to feel him within her.

But he wouldn't cooperate.

He raised her dress, and slid down her body, his teeth nipping at her flesh. Then he was between her thighs, and he used his finger tracing back and forth over her damp folds. She arched, a scream building in her throat. He removed his hand, and replaced it with his mouth, sucking against her with the same hard intensity he'd done at her breast.

Sheldon beat at the sand, her body strung tight like a bow. The orgasm coming now, riding over her in waves.

After she came, she dug her hands into the skin of his back, wanting him to slide up, wanting to feel him inside her.

He raised his head, looked at her face, and then shook his head. "No."

"What do you mean, no?"

"You're going to pay, Sheldon."

And then he lowered his head, his mouth once again at her clit. Oh, please, no. It was too soon. Already the pressure was more insistent than before. Her hands dug into his back, his arms, needing him to slow down. But he was beyond listening to her, beyond listening to reason.

He kept up the torture, his hands cupping her rear, keeping her there, and she could feel herself coming once again. It started between her thighs, her legs stiffening, her toes curling into the sand, her whole body rising to meet the pressure.

She began to mutter. Nonsense, because her brain had stopped.

"Can you think?" he asked.

Her head moved from one side to the other. "No," she cried.

"Good. I don't want you to think. I can't think. I don't want you to think, either."

And then he shifted higher up her body, freed his cock from his briefs, and jammed himself inside her.

It wasn't done with finesse.

This wasn't about performance.

This was something else.

He levered his hands on either side of her head, his cock moving in and out, faster and faster, harder and deeper.

At first the rough friction hurt, but then her body began to adjust, began to react. She locked her legs around his hips, and moved, her hips working to keep up the fast rhythm he was setting, until they were moving together, flesh slapping against flesh, and Sheldon knew she wasn't going to survive this. No woman could survive this battle. And that's what it was. This wasn't sex, this was war.

Her thighs tightened around him, constricting, and she heard his gasp. Each time he pounded, she tightened again, his breathing coming quick and hard.

Her head was feeling lighter and lighter still, until there was no more air left to breath.

Sheldon screamed.

His body froze, poised above her, and he jerked once, twice. His head listed back, the sweat on his chest glistening in the moonlight.

Never had she seen him like this. More of an animal than a man.

Sheldon smiled at the sight. Raw, real.

So this was life. It was good.

JEFF COLLAPSED ON THE SAND, pushing his hair back from his face.

His heart was still racing. Partially from sex, partially from fear.

My God.

He wanted to look at her, stare, drink her in, but he was afraid she'd see too much, and he wasn't going to let that happen.

But there was one thing he needed to discuss, right now. "We never had sex before."

She looked over at him, her hair tangled from his hands, her dress bunched around her waist. She didn't look like Sheldon Summerville—billionairess, shopping connoisseur—she looked like nothing more than the girl next door. A well-tossed girl next door…and his brain started to quit on him.

He shook his head.

"What do you mean?" she asked.

"You told me that we'd slept together. I would remember this."

She sat upright, her eyes warm and womanly. "Because it was so good?"

"Because…it doesn't matter why. I just know that I've never, ever, been inside you before now."

She lay back down, moonlight easing over her breasts, shimmering on the damp, golden skin between her thighs. "It was good."

"Don't get all full of yourself," he said.

"I thought you'd be different."

"Different from what?"

"You were kinda wild, there. I don't know, I thought you'd be like, "Oh, baby, baby, I love the way your breasts feel, baby.""

He turned away from her, watched the waves, hurt by the teasing tone. "I didn't know you were disappointed."

Something must have come through in his voice, because she sat up abruptly and put a hand on his chest. "You don't understand. That's what I loved about it. You were real. That wasn't a performance. That was you, wasn't it?"

Her face was soft, still flushed and glowing, and he wasn't going to lie. "Yeah."

She curled up next to him, her curves fitting against him. "It was nice," she whispered.

Automatically he began to stroke her hair. He shouldn't be doing crap like that. Intimate stuff, but he needed to touch her. The chances of this happening again were almost zero; they both knew it, or at least he did. Sheldon would always have a problem with the rules.

"Jeff?" she asked, her voice catching on his name. He

knew there were questions she wanted to ask, solutions that he didn't have, solutions to her life that he would never have.

Instead of answering her, he leaned over, kissed her with all his unspent desire.

Her hand slid down to cup his erection, her small fingers working magic on his skin. She stroked him once, twice, and then she glided down his body, her breasts flowing over him like wine, and then her mouth closed over his cock, and Jeff forgot whatever questions she wanted to ask. He forgot about everything but this.

THE FIREWORKS WERE OVER. ALL the big, bright bursts of color were packed away until next year. Sheldon watched as Jeff pulled on his clothes, his face set in a hard line. No joy there. All that was left was three used condoms, just another night of sex on the beach.

And her ripped-out heart. A useless organ, highly overrated, which she swore she could see lying washed up in the surf.

Only a man would take earth-shattering sex and ruin the afterglow.

Only Jeff could make her cry about it.

Sheldon wiped at her face.

"This was a mistake, wasn't it?" she asked, pulling her dress over her head. The dress was pretty much ruined, but she really didn't want to be naked in front of him again.

"Yeah."

"I'm good at mistakes," she tried, and he didn't disagree. She could still taste him in her mouth, on her tongue. Beer, the salt of his skin, the salt of his sex. Sheldon closed her eyes, trying to shut out the pain.

"Sheldon, sex muddies up a lot of things. Makes things look different, better than they are. I didn't want this to happen." He stood up, brushing the sand off his clothes. Why didn't this bother him? He should look hurt, dejected, depressed. Instead, his face expression was the same as if he'd just come in from a rough game of golf.

"You shouldn't have let this happen because it might look better than it is?" she said, not trying to keep the sarcasm out of her voice.

"Yeah."

Sheldon studied the calming waters of the ocean and took a deep breath. All she could smell was the painful aftermath of sex when the consequences come into play. Now every time she looked at the sea, every time she smelled the salt air, she'd only remember the feel of him moving inside her, under a summer's moon. She'd remember the touch of his bare skin underneath her fingers and the hot desperation in his kiss, a kiss she could have sworn was real. He had ruined this for her.

Bastard.

"We need to be getting back. Your date, your parents, somebody will be looking for you," he said, dismissing her, moving on as if this was nothing. As if she was nothing.

Nuh-uh.

"Give me a minute, huh?" she asked, tucking her skirt around her waist and wading thigh-deep into the water. The ocean was cold, but she didn't mind. It rushed over her, flowed in her. "I have to get clean." Then she waded back out, adjusting her dress and giving him her happiest smile.

His mouth was one thin line, his eyes black as the

night. "Don't be mad at me because you can't stand up to your father."

"That is such a low thing to say, Jeff. This is all my fault?"

"I'm not the one getting married."

"I bet you like that I'm getting married. No commitment here. Just screw her and then when she's married, no muss, no fuss, no messy clean-up necessary. Do you want to meet my other friends who are about to get engaged?"

"You're just mad right now," he said, turning away from her.

"Damn straight, I'm mad right now. You're a coward, Jeff Brooks."

That brought him around. He came up, stood in front of her, his jaw tight with anger. "You're calling me a coward? Look in the mirror, babe."

"You know you were my one friend. I liked you. I *liked* you," she said, and because she couldn't bear it anymore, she picked up her phone because she was going to need a ride home after all. Before she could flip it open, she noticed two people walking toward her.

"Woo-hoo!!! Shell! It's your…sister!"

And so it was. Cami—and Lance.

A heavily intoxicated Cami and Lance. Cami had traded in heels for pink flip-flips and Sheldon got her first good look at the love of Cami's life. A hipster, wouldn't you know it?

He had a tattoo on one arm, a fledgling goatee, and sideburns not seen since Elvis was alive.

"Jeff, meet my sister, Cami. Cami, this is Jeff."

Cami smiled. "He's hot. Not as hot as my Lance

here," she said, waving a bottle of champagne in Lance's direction, "but still pretty hot."

Sheldon gave Lance a warm, deserving smile—hoping Jeff would notice. "Good to meet you. I've heard a lot about you."

Right then Sheldon's phone rang. Caller ID said Mom.

Sheldon answered. "Hi, Mom. What's up?"

"I'm looking for your sister."

"Cami? I think she already left," she said, staring at her sister, who was slightly teetering on the sand.

"I'm worried, Sheldon. We can't find her."

"I'm sure she's fine, Mom. She told me she was leaving early to head back to the city."

"Yes, but she got in a car…"

"Well, there you go."

"With a strange man. And tattoos. Perhaps your father and I should return to Charles's place?"

"Don't worry."

"I want to make sure she's okay. There was that murder in Sag Harbor last week."

"She's not with a murderer," muttered Sheldon. "Hold on a minute, Mom…"

Sheldon muted her cell and looked over at her sister, who was grinning happily, completely oblivious to all the problems she was causing. Their mother wouldn't quit until she talked to Cami…unless she had something new and even worse to occupy her mind. If there was one thing Sheldon could do well, it was "worse."

"Cami, you and Lance head to—" she looked up the beach "—the Howards. Theirs is the Cape Cod two places over. Blue, white trim, very cute. Do you remember?"

"It's a little late to be crashing in uninvited, Sheldon?"

"No, I don't expect you to show up at the door, don't be a doofus. Head for the guesthouse, the key's under the flower pot, it's usually azaleas or something big and poufy."

"You know all this, how?" asked Jeff.

"I dated their son three summers ago."

His eyebrows came together. "Doesn't bother me. Doesn't bother me. Doesn't bother me."

She wasn't going to deal with him now. Couldn't. The hurt inside was her was too new. Instead, she turned to her sister. "Go," she ordered, pointing up the beach.

Cami and Lance began walking toward the house, and Sheldon unmuted her phone. "She's fine Mom. That was her lab partner with the tattoos. I'm sure of it. And uh, so are the people I'm with," she said.

"Are you sure, Sheldon? Besides, we could collect you, as well."

"Don't worry, Mom. Somebody said they were driving back tonight," she said, hoping, praying that that would be enough.

"We'll come along by the beach. Just in case…"

And no, it wasn't.

"No, you can't!!!" she yelled, earning a concerned look from Jeff.

"Sheldon?" said her Mother.

Sheldon glanced at Jeff, who was watching her, arms folded across his chest, serenely observing her life like he didn't have a care.

She wanted to hurt him like he had hurt her, to strike back and see if he would bleed like other people did. The phone burned in her hand, and she realized that revenge was in her grasp. She could make him pay. She wanted to make him pay. If she were a stronger person, maybe she would, but she cared, and she hated herself for caring.

"Sheldon?"

"Wait a minute, Mom," she said, muting the phone once more. She turned to Jeff, and nodded in the direction of Cami and Lance. "Help them. Cami's having trouble. What if she ends up at the wrong house?"

"Your sister's an adult."

"She's my sister," she argued back. "My parent's think she's an angel. They're not going to be disillusioned about both daughters. Go," she ordered, because she needed him out of here. Fast.

"I don't feel right about this."

"Now, you get feelings? I don't want to know this. I can't do this. Go."

He started to argue again, but then shook it off. "Fine," he agreed, and trekked upward in the curlicue path of Cami and Lance. She watched him until he was safely out of range.

"Mom?"

"Sheldon? What's going on? Is someone else there?"

"Oh, yeah, lots of people," answered Sheldon,

Sheldon made assorted whooping noises, creating an imaginary party, immensely glad that no one was around to witness this low moment in Sheldon's life, which was saying quite a bit.

She began to slur her words. "Listen, Mom, uh, this conversation has really been nice and pleasant, really nice and pleasant, I always love talking to you, really, but I really need tooo…ah, go…"

"Sheldon, are you drunk?"

"Just r-r-r-r-right down the beach. I'm fine, Mom, really! Peachy!"

"I'm coming to get you, Sheldon. This is it."

And finally the reaction that she needed. "Sure, Mom." Sheldon hung up, threw the two beer bottles on the sand. It would have been more convenient if Jeff was the super-size party animal type, but she'd deal. Then she started weaving back and forth in to the waves, completely soaking the bottom of her dress.

God, what a girl had to do to get attention in this town.

Finally, she spotted a flashlight coming down the beach, pointed in her direction. Sheldon waved wildly, staggering a little more.

At last the cavalry had arrived. Mom was there, resplendent in her white cocktail trouser set, complete with the diamond necklace and tennis bracelet, and Wayne was huffing a few hundred feet back.

"Sheldon, who else is here with you?" asked her mother in her mother voice.

Sheldon waved off into the distance. "Bye! It was…fabulous."

"Who is that?" asked her mother, pointing up to the top of the dunes.

Sheldon followed her mother's finger.

Damn. Damn. Damn.

Slowly Jeff approached the beach, a pulse ticking in his jaw. He glanced over her wet clothes, and looked at her with angry frustration in his eyes. It wasn't the emotion she wanted to see, but at least Teflon-man was feeling something.

"This is your fault," her mother announced, glaring at Jeff.

Jeff glanced at Sheldon, and she knew he was waiting to see what she'd say. Once again, an opportunity to get even for his rejection was hers for the taking. Once again, an opportunity lost.

"Stefan was here, Mom. He met me." She squinted in Jeff's general direction. "Who are you?" It wasn't an Oscar-worthy performance, but Sheldon thought it was pretty good.

Wayne Summerville came to a halt beside them. "Cynthia, did you find Cami?" He looked at Sheldon, looked at Jeff. "Well, well, look what the cat dragged in." Her father turned to Jeff. "You got her in this condition? Sorry, Mr. Brooks. You're fired."

8

MONDAY MORNING WAS AN EXERCISE in humility for Jeff. Columbia-Starr operated behind closed doors. There were no reprimands, no lectures, no marks on your permanent record. Instead, one day you represented one of the largest consumer product accounts in America, and the next, you were hawking diet products to focus groups in Staten Island.

Yet the upside to ThinLife diet products was that he longer had to watch Sheldon Summerville, no longer had to fight the urge to keep from touching her, no longer had to catch his breath when she smiled in his direction. No, ThinLife was definitely a good thing.

He had lunch with the company's CEO, an elegant woman who had lost over 300 pounds and showed him before-and-after pictures like a proud parent showing off her kids. Jeff listened attentively, made notes when she listed her goals for the new product campaign, and had only one momentary lapse when a blonde in the corner cocked her head in a familiar fashion. Just a false alarm but enough to make him mad.

What sort of idiot daydreams about the woman who got him fired from the sweetest gig he'd ever had? Who took his dream of owning a boat and crashed it against the rocks? And okay, he might have been partially responsible here, but it was easier to pretend to hate her than to contemplate anything more.

And for Jeff, the easy way was always the best way.

Actually, the day was moving along okay until quitting time, when Jeff was packing up to leave, and Phil came into the office.

"I got you something," said Phil. "I'm sorry about the Summerville account," he said, slipping a package onto Jeff's desk before leaving the room.

Jeff opened up the box. It was a tie. Black with blue stripes. Conservative, staid, boring. Jeff looked at the tie, considered chunking it into the trash but realized that now that he represented ThinLife, he was going to need black ties with blue stripes. It was with a heavy heart that he put the tie in his backpack and walked away from the office, head bowed low.

He spent the evening reviewing the campaign for promoting ThinLife's new diet shake, actually drank one for dinner, all in the pursuit of vigorously representing his client. Regrettably, it tasted like chocolate-flavoured mud, which meant Jeff was going to have to work hard. Very hard.

On Tuesday, he arranged an appearance on *The Today Show* for the ThinLife CEO and spent the afternoon preparing for the next afternoon's events. Right before he was leaving, his sister stopped by the office, in the guise of asking for help but mainly because she had a perverse need to make everyone's life hell.

She burst in, a vision in a T-shirt ripped at the stomach, and in a black leather biker cap. Jeff winced.

"Why are you here?" He wanted to know.

"Why are you wearing a gimme cap?" she countered. Jeff raised a hand to his head, and remembered that in the spirit of vigorously representing his client, he was still wearing the ThinLife cap from the earlier television gig. Quickly, he swiped it off his head, but the damage was done.

Her dark eyes narrowed, nostrils flaring as she sensed her prey's weakened state. "What happened?" she asked.

"Nothing," said Jeff, removing the ThinLife PR materials from the range of her eagle-eye vision.

"Why are you looking at brochures on diet shakes?"

"I got another assignment. One of the guys went on vacation, so I was asked to take over for a few days. You know, company man, team player, rah, rah, that's me."

She fell into the chair across from his desk and rested her hands on her stomach, fingers intertwined. "I need your assistance," she said.

A bullet dodged. Jeff gave her a smile full of brotherly love. "What can I do for you, sis?"

"That op-ed piece for the *Times* that you promised me. I want something provocative, witty, sexy and intelligent. It definitely needs to be intelligent."

"You're the writer. Write it."

"I'm not a hack, Jeff. I'm an artist. A free spirit, unhampered by the constraints of a conservative culture that wants to set the clock back fifty years. Before the days of Madonna or Janet Jackson or South Park. I want this country to be free."

Jeff started to laugh.

"It's not funny."

"Okay, besides, I owe you anyway."

She raised a brow. "Why?"

"You didn't run the pictures from the strike in *The Red Choo Diaries*. I thought you would jump at the opportunity."

"Why do you consistently underestimate my ethical principles?"

"Would you like a list?"

"Oh! Is this the punishment I get for being nice and respecting my brother's precarious relationship with his client?"

Jeff knew he was beaten, so he held up his hands. "You're right. You're right." She laid out her points efficiently and Jeff made some notes. Within an hour, she had her response. Provocative, witty, sexy, intelligent and, in general, freaking great. Jeff was good, if not great at spinning shit into gold. He saved the file on a thumb drive and handed it to her. "You owe me," he stated.

Mercedes looked at him skeptically.

"We're even," he clarified and she nodded.

"So what's going on with Sheldon?" she asked.

"What do you mean?" he said cautiously.

"It's a simple question, what do you not understand about it?"

"I don't understand anything about it. I think you need to clarify what you are asking," he said, pretending to paw through his desk drawer.

Unfortunately, Mercedes knew him too well. "You got fired from the account, didn't you?"

"Did not," he said.

"What's her social program for tonight?"

Anything but missing him. Knowing Sheldon, nudity

would be involved as well. Jeff gave his sister his best PR smile. "Sitting at home, alone."

She pointed an accusing finger at him. "Aha! Not true."

And wouldn't that be just like Sheldon? To run to Mercedes, simply to make his life an even more hellish hell. Actually, it wasn't anything like Sheldon, Jeff knew it, but his mind was still bleeding from the idea of Sheldon sharing her nudity with anybody else.

"I don't care what she's doing tonight, or who she's doing it to. If she sent you to rub my nose in it, to hell with that."

"There's something for me to rub your nose in? Share, darling brother." Mercedes' eyes narrowed, closing in for the kill.

Jeff looked up and saw the feral gleam in her eye. He considered trying to explain, considered a flat-out lie.

He ended up looking at his watch. "I have a meeting in five. Gotta go."

He rose from his desk, stuffed some papers into a pack, waved to Phil on the way out and ran, never once looking back.

MERCEDES LAUGHED SOFTLY TO herself, watching her brother run for his life. There was a story here. A scandal of epic proportions, and probably, knowing Jeff, it involved sex. The wild-child socialite taming the roguish playboy with her pole-dancing ways.

Nah.

Maybe the bad boy finally losing his heart to the one woman who had a lower moral code than him, his heart trampled by her red, do-me stiletto heels?

Mercedes shook her head. *No.*

The carefree bachelor terrified by the idea of committing to one woman for the next six weeks, much less the rest of his life?

Yup. That was the one.

So what would the wild-child socialite think about all this? How would she react? Suicidal? Depressed, acting out her anger and rage by screwing every man on the planet?

Mercedes steepled her fingers, seeing a wealth of plot possibilities unfolding before her. Any number of them that would shoot her blog to the number one spot on the charts. The diaries had taken off beyond what she had imagined, she'd landed an agent, and was currently polishing up a book proposal. The fates of the publishing world were finally working with her, which was good, but even more interesting was what had happened with Jeff and Sheldon, and there was only one way to find out.

She picked up a piece of paper off his desk, and walked out to talk to Phil.

"So, Phil, listen, Jeff asked me to drop this off at Miss Summerville's house, but he tore out of here before I could get the address, and now, I don't know, his cell keeps kicking over to voice mail. Can you help me out here?" She batted her eyelashes. "Please."

"He can't bear to face her, can he?"

Instantly, Mercedes put on a look of sincere understanding and sisterly commiseration. "You know?" she said.

Phil nodded.

"How was he today?"

Phil pursed his mouth. "Good. Such a brave little soldier. You know, around here, they don't flush things out in the open, let people vent. It all gets built up inside, repressed, completely unhealthy. All that whispering…"

"Whispering?" asked Mercedes with genuine concern. "Are they whispering about my brother? I can't bear to see him go through this. How's he been? Really?"

"Yesterday was very hard," answered Phil. "He didn't snap at me like normal. Even told me that he liked my jacket. I nearly cried."

"Did you see Sheldon on Monday?"

"Oh, no, the Summervilles haven't come near this place," he whispered. "It's like nuclear fallout."

Mercedes seated herself across from Phil and leaned her chin on her hand. "I know that Jeff appreciates what you're doing. He speaks highly of you."

"He does?"

Mercedes nodded once. "I don't know what they were thinking…"

"Do you know what happened?" asked Phil, his blue eyes wide. "No one knows all the details."

Mercedes closed her eyes and rubbed the bridge of her nose. "I can't say, and you know, Jeff, he's so private, he won't tell you what he's thinking or what he's feeling, anyway."

Phil nodded. "I know. I've tried to get him to open up, too. Stress is so hard on the heart. It'll rip years off his life expectancy."

Mercedes patted Phil's hand. "Thank you. Thank you for being here and supporting him. You don't know what that means to me, to all of the family." Then she sniffed, clasping her hand to her heart.

"Anything that I can do," answered Phil.

"Sheldon's address?" asked Mercedes.

"Of course," Phil said.

Mercedes took the address and brushed a tear from her eye. "I don't know what to say," she told him.

"It's all right, honey. Just go home and have a good cry. You'll feel better."

SHELDON SUMMERVILLE'S APARTMENT was pretty fancy. Not nearly as chic-chic as what Mercedes expected, but it didn't matter. Sheldon invited her in, and Mercedes settled herself on the couch, trying not to admire the careless arrangement of throw pillows that were scattered around, nor the cute flowered couch with yellow trim. All tastefully done. But she wasn't here for decorating tips. She was here about the story. Roiling human emotions and possibly a broken heart, possibly her brother's. Mercedes narrowed her eyes and gave Sheldon her best death stare. Having two older brothers, she had mastered the death stare at an early age.

"Look, bitch. You don't mind if I call you bitch, do you?"

Sheldon blinked once, and Mercedes knew she had her right where she wanted her.

"I know you live here in your fancy apartment, with your fancy genuine Prada bag, and those killer red Manolo's, but you know, that isn't what counts in life. Do you know what counts? How you treat people. What goes around is going to come back and bite you right in that gold-plated ass of yours."

Sheldon blinked once again, and those innocent blue eyes didn't look as if they held a single clue.

"You sound upset," Sheldon said. "Am I supposed to follow this?"

Mercedes sighed. This was going to be more difficult than she'd thought. "I don't let anybody walk all over my brother," she said flatly, eyeing the aquamarine top that Sheldon was wearing and wondering if it was a genuine Elie Tahari.

"I didn't do anything to your brother."

"Oh, yeah, and I suppose that's why he got fired?"

"From Columbia-Starr?"

"Well, no, from the Summerville Consumer Products account."

"Oh."

It was a heckuva lot harder prying secrets out of Sheldon. The woman was like a clam. Mercedes deepened her scowl. "That's all you're going to say is 'oh'? You trample all over someone with those cool shoes and all you can say is 'oh'?"

"So what," said Sheldon, picking up a throw pillow and cradling it against her.

So Sheldon was the trampler and Jeff the tramplee? Now Mercedes got seriously mad. Nobody messed with her brothers. Nobody. "I don't like you, and I thought I was going to. You made Jeff behave even dopier than he normally does, and I admired that about you."

"I did that?" Sheldon asked carefully, her fingers playing with the pillow trim in a telling movement that hid a troubled emotional state. *So the heartless hussy wasn't so heartless after all.* Mercedes softened her approach. "You know you did," said Mercedes. "If you could see him now, just a shadow of the man that he was."

Sheldon looked up, and the fingers stayed still. "I don't believe that." No longer was she wearing that "nobody's home" look in her eyes. No, the wheels were starting to turn in that not-so-empty blond head. Time to pry more.

"It's true. You know where he is right now? At home, drunk as a skunk, hasn't shaved in days. All he can do is stare into space, with this sad expression in his eyes. Defeated."

"Jeff?"

Mercedes nodded.

Sheldon's mouth formed an angry line, and her fingers started playing on the pillow again. "He deserved it. The bastard."

Aha. Now they were getting to the heart of the matter. "You were mad at him?"

Sheldon nodded. "I probably shouldn't have done it, but I needed to help out Cami."

"Cami?"

"My younger sister. You know, Mom and Dad think they know what's best, and so she doesn't want them to know about Lance."

"Lance?"

"Her boyfriend. He has a tattoo that goes all they way down his arm. Between that and the band…"

"Ahhh…"

"And I honestly didn't think Dad would fire the firm. I thought I could talk my way out of it. I tried."

"So your dad was really mad?" asked Mercedes.

"Oh, yeah, he was furious. Mom was running interference all day on Sunday. He wouldn't even speak to me."

"Hmm," said Mercedes, nodding appropriately.

"If Josh hadn't been there…"

"Josh?"

"My fiancé."

"You're engaged?" Mercedes tried not to look disapproving, but an engagement threw a different light on the situation. Maybe Jeff had walked away because Sheldon was promised to another man. Jeff? Her lacking-moral-value brother?

"Not yet." Sheldon waved a careless hand. "It's a business thing."

"Oh," answered Mercedes wisely, glad to know the true state of affairs. If she wasn't engaged yet, Jeff would've jumped all over that. "And when you and Jeff…. Then Josh got really mad?"

"Josh doesn't care. All he wants is to see Con-Mason U.S.A. hit the Fortune Top 500."

Mercedes didn't care about Con-Mason, she wanted the straight skinny on what was going on. "But when you and Jeff…then *somebody* got mad?"

"Nobody knows about Jeff," said Sheldon. "Not even Cami. You know, I wanted to tell her, to talk to somebody, but the only person I've *ever* been able to talk to is your brother and he doesn't care about me. I'm just a notch in his beer wall."

For the first time, Mercedes noticed the hurt in Sheldon's eyes. This obviously wasn't Jeff's casual one-night stand. Mercedes remembered how angry he'd been at the office, the hurt (according to Phil) he'd suffered in silence. Man, these two headstrong kids were totally screwed up. "I don't think Jeff has a beer wall," said Mercedes, trying to cheer Sheldon up. "So, what *did* you do that made your father so mad?"

And Sheldon told her about the entire night, well, except for the part about where she and Jeff… Mercedes made her skip that part, because Mercedes couldn't really handle details, and she knew enough about biology.

Eventually, the whole sordid picture emerged, a TeleNova soap opera right in her own neighborhood.

Jeff was in a shitload of trouble. Sheldon had a thing for him, but he was doing the whole "I'm a jerk" routine (which he did really well), and Mercedes thought she could spin off an entire sex-in-the-Hamptons series for *The Red Choo Diaries.*

That would be extremely fabulous.

But first she needed to get back Jeff's client. Mercedes loved her brothers, especially Jeff because sometimes Andrew was a real stick-in-the-mud, although to be fair, she loved him, too. And although she would never tell him, Jeff was a good guy, and he needed this account, because he needed to buy his boat so that Mercedes could go out riding in it and meet all the cute guys that hung out at the docks. No, Jeff definitely needed to get Summerville Consumer Products back as a client, and he wouldn't have the brains to do it. This job took creativity, a keen eye for human behavior, a touch of the dramatic and, probably, definitely, a starring role for *The Red Choo Diaries.*

Mercedes rubbed her hands together. "You know that you have to make this right," she told Sheldon.

Sheldon blinked a couple of times. Jeez, it was like Morse code or something, but then she nodded.

"You care for Jeff, and he's not a jerk. Well, not all the time. Sometimes he's, like, okay. But only sometimes, and then, you know—"

"It's okay," Sheldon interrupted. "I'll do whatever needs to be done."

"We need to get your father to rehire Jeff."

Sheldon looked skeptical, never having been exposed to Mercedes's capabilities. "He'll never do it."

Mercedes smiled slowly. "Never say never to a member of the Brooks' family. Well, it's me and Mom who you don't want to say 'never' to. My brothers... well, you know sometimes they—"

"What are you thinking?" asked Sheldon, interrupting again.

"You got any wine around here? I think this is going to take awhile."

9

"Boss?"

Jeff looked up to see Phil peeking into the office. "What is it?"

"I didn't want to tell you, and, I don't want to see you upset either."

Sensing forthcoming disaster and because he'd had a lot of disasters in his life recently, Jeff put down his pen so he wouldn't be tempted to stick it through his eye. "What is it?"

"You promise you won't let this upset you?"

"I don't think I need to promise," answered Jeff.

"You need to promise."

Jeff exhaled heavily. "All right. I promise."

Phil closed his eyes and stuck out a sheet of paper. "I printed it for you." Then he sniffed and ran out.

Jeff stared at the paper, his mouth going dry.

The Red Choo Diaries.

Slowly, because he knew this couldn't be good, he began to read:

It all started on a starry Saturday night in Southampton when the fireworks were booming overhead. A certain blond-haired, blue-eyed heiress with a randy reputation, we'll call her Mandy Mega-licious, had been the object of carnal knowledge from a certain playboy of international original, we'll just call him Randy.

Randy was a dark-haired, fiery-eyed Casanova with a voracious taste for the ladies, and Mandy was his current dietary requirement.

The evening had started out tamely enough, when the two found themselves alone on a dark, secluded strip of beach, and soon the fireworks really began.

Mandy had worn a white Oscar de la Renta for the event, but the flimsy garment was history under the strength of Randy's hot-blooded hands. Soon, the comely siren was bare in the sand, lying anxiously for her lover, wanting to discover if all the rumors about his fevered lovemaking were true.

Carelessly he tossed the black tuxedo jacket into the sand. His shirt was stark white, a sharp contrast to the tanned harshness of his face. In the moonlight, his dark eyes glittered with promise of a night full of hot, Latin love. She watched him undress, an explosion of color lighting up the sky. She wet her lips as he removed his shirt, and she saw the sculpted muscles that were awaiting her touch. She'd been with men before, but never with one so…big. He watched her pale skin in the dark, a smile on his face.

Her face was flushed, fevered from desire as he put his mouth to her breast, using tongue and teeth to coax the rosy peak into a tight bud that made her gasp with desire.

"I want you to touch yourself," he told her in a voice that brooked no argument. Not if she wanted to sample the hard ridge that was easily visible beneath the black trousers.

Overhead in the sky, a bright burst of yellow sparkled through the night, and her thighs parted, her golden curls already damp with longing. The teasing and toying touches of the night had kindled a blaze inside her, and her fuse was short. Her hand was shaking, but she obeyed the command, touching a finger to the edge of her lips. She was slick, her flesh swollen with desire.

"How does it feel?" he asked, his eyes locked with hers.

Mandy arched her hips and her finger skated briefly over her aching clit. "Good," she answered, her breath catching from the effort of trying to speak.

He seated himself on the sand next to her, one hand reaching out to stroke the soft flesh of her belly. Back and forth he traced, whisper-light, more than a tickle but providing no satisfaction, only fuel to the flame.

She began to trace back and forth along her slit, trying to keep the touches light and harmless, but the passion in his eyes made that impossible. Slowly, lasciviously, her finger grew bolder, her tiny nubbin pulsing with each flick of her finger.

"You do this often?" he asked, quirking an eyebrow, as if he were discussing the weather.

She wanted to lie to him, but couldn't, and nodded her head once with shame.

His finger traced upward, circling a nipple, as if to reward her honesty.

Mandy wanted his fingers to stay, begged and pleaded with him, but he laughed as if he could read her mind, and his hand moved lower, yet not low enough.

"It is up to you to pleasure yourself, not me," he said.

Mandy arched her back and closed her eyes, pretending that she was alone, pretending that he wasn't there to see her bare and open.

But Randy didn't like that. He positioned himself between her thighs, pulling them wide over his legs. She could feel the crisp hairs of his legs tickling her skin, felt the tight strength of the muscles in his calves, in his thighs. She longed to feel more, but he stayed her hand when it moved toward him.

"No, no, no," he answered.

Mandy gritted her teeth because she could see the swollen length of his cock hoarded between his legs, and she wanted to feel it inside her.

"After you come, you can have a sample, love," he whispered, and his hand moved from her belly to her arm to trace over her mouth.

She took his finger in his mouth and began to suck hard, letting him feel her anger and frustration.

Randy merely laughed.

Her other hand moved faster inside her, inside her folds, slick and wet, sending sharp electrical jolts to her body. She wanted him inside her, wanted to feel the thick length, and if she closed her eyes, she could already feel him. Faster she went, the shocks coming quickly now, and she knew her climax was near. Her hips rose off the sand, her mind exploding like the fireworks overhead. Her breathing came faster, until finally, with a single gasp, she lay back on the sand.

She opened her eyes and at him.

"I think there's something you owe me," she told me.

Randy took her finger in his mouth and traced her juices with his tongue. And with one easy stroke inside her, he began to fulfill his part of the bargain.

It was worse.

Jeff picked up his pen, examining its usefulness as an instrument of death. In the end he decided that mere pen-stabbing would be too painless for Mercedes.

He picked up the phone and punched in her cell number.

Voice mail.

"Mercedes, this is Jeff. Got a lead on that Op-Ed for the *Times*. Call me."

Then he dialed her apartment.

Answering machine.

"Mercedes, this is Jeff. Guess what? I ran into a guy from, uh, some publishing house. They love your stuff. Call me."

He called his mother next.

"Mom, have you talked to Mercedes today?"

"No, I haven't. Not today. I've been meaning to call her."

"Any idea where she is?"

"Probably at home. Have you tried there?"

"Yes, Mom," answered Jeff, twisting the phone cord and considering the merits of death by strangulation.

"Is it something important? Can I help you with it?"

"No, it's nothing important I know her birthday is coming up, and I thought I'd ask—"

"Her birthday is in January."

"That far off? Wow, the short-term memory really goes after thirty."

"It's all that alcohol you're consuming, not your age."

"Alcohol does not kill brain cells."

"Well, be careful, and don't let the cops get involved. Celeste Mahoney's son got arrested just last week for public intoxication. Very sad. She's beside herself. I'm going to make some lasagna to take over there on Sunday. Poor Celeste. I don't want anyone making lasagna for me, Jeff. Capiche?"

"Yes, Mom."

"I love you, Jeff. Remember, stay out of trouble."

"Love you, too," he said and hung up.

The only other option was Andrew, and Jeff had to weigh his fear that Andrew actually read Mercedes' blog and might recognize the parties involved against the steely anger that was wrapped around him like a snake.

Finally he picked up the phone.

"Andrew, yeah, it's Jeff."

"Jeff who?"

"Your brother Jeff. Don't be a smart-ass. Listen, have you talked to Mercedes? I've been trying to get in touch with her."

"You tried her cell?"

Jeff sighed extra heavily so Andrew could hear. "Yeah, I tried the cell. Tried her apartment, too. No luck."

"What're you looking for Mercedes for?" Andrew asked, and Jeff could hear that note of interest in his voice. He knew something.

"No reason, I just wanted to chat with her."

"Surf the Web today, little brother?"

Andrew knew. Jeff decided to play dumb. "I haven't seen anything. Too busy."

"*The Red Choo Diaries* has a great piece of literary

erotica on one blond bombshell and her Hamptons' date last Saturday night. Sounded just like you and Sheldon. We're running an office pool on the identity of the guy. Odds for you are three–two."

"How does your office know who I am?"

"I told them."

Jeff made an obscene gesture at the phone receiver. "Couldn't be me, I was home alone on Saturday."

"Don't lie to me, Jeff. We all know it was you. And it's only a matter of time before names are revealed, videos pop up on the Internet, and women start throwing vibrators in your direction."

"I really don't like you, Andrew."

"What cums around, gets around."

"I am not Randy," he said tightly.

Andrew was laughing too hard to say anything.

"That's really not funny, Andrew. I didn't laugh when it happened to you and Jamie. I distinctly remember feeling sympathy, deep sympathy, for you. Remember that next time you need a favor from me."

"Go shopping with me tomorrow."

"Can't. Got something to do."

"Does it involve sex on the beach?"

Jeff didn't want to think about sex on the beach. Mercedes' story was off the mark, but he'd avoided thinking about that night because it had been too heart-pounding, too soul-stirring. Jeff could cope with the all-powerful properties of great sex, but soul-stirring terrified him. His soul didn't stir. Ever. And if Sheldon wasn't Sheldon, *maybe* he'd think about stirred souls. *If* she didn't have more money than Andrew, *if* she wasn't engaged to be married—almost engaged—*if* she

didn't display her charms for the entire planet to view—
and most of all, *if* she'd ever said one word about her
feelings for him.

"Jeff, can you hear me now?"

Jeff shook off all thoughts of stirred souls. "What?"

"What are you doing tomorrow?"

"I have a shake-off."

"What's a shake-off?"

"You don't want to know."

"Yeah, yes, I do."

"Diet products. The best shake recipe wins an all-
expense paid trip to Paris, plus a new wardrobe."

"Wow."

"Don't be an ass."

"I said 'wow,' what's wrong with that?"

"I heard the sarcasm in that 'wow.'"

"Sorry."

"Apology accepted."

"But you can go out afterward? This shake-off won't
last forever, will it?"

Jeff decided that maybe it would be good to be
around Andrew. His brother was grounded and rational, both of which seemed to be qualities missing in
his life right now. "Yeah, we could do that. Where do
you want to go?"

"Shopping."

"I know that. But for what? You don't shop. That
would involve spending money."

Andrew said something particularly vile that involved physical impossibilities.

"Does your girlfriend know you talk like that?"

"She likes it when I talk like that."

"Way too personal, dude. Be at Rockefeller Center at 2:30."

"Sure, Randy."

Jeff slammed down the phone.

BY FOUR-THIRTY THAT AFTERNOON, Mercedes, probably fearing for her life, still hadn't called back. Jeff picked up the phone to call Sheldon, but kept putting it down. He didn't want to hear her voice, didn't want her to linger over his name. No, that chapter was closed. She was used to being tabloid fodder and one more story wasn't going to bother her at all.

Jeff walked outside his office, where Phil was manning the lobby.

"I need a favor, Phil."

"Anything," he answered.

"Don't get your hopes up."

Phil smirked. "Ah, the ogre has returned. Glad you're feeling better."

"I need you to call Mercedes."

"Your sister?"

"She's not returning my calls, and I don't think she'd take a call from the office, either. It's an emergency. You can use my cell and we'll block the number."

Phil took the phone. "A RAZR, very stylish."

Jeff nodded curtly. "You're going to have to say you're Johnny D'Amato."

Phil picked up his pen and began to write. "How does Johnny sound? And is it Johnny, or John?"

"It's Johnny, and he sounds like a man."

"Bass or tenor voice?"

"Average."

"Accent."

"Average."

"You're not making this any fun," said Phil.

Jeff took a deep, calming breath. "All you have to tell her is that you're in town for the day on business and you'd like to see her tonight."

"What if she says no?"

"This is Johnny D'Amato. She'll move mountains to see him again."

"Am I married?"

"Tell her you're divorced."

"Should I make it a difficult divorce?"

"Phil, can we just call?"

"Oh, fine Mr. Fuddy Duddy."

Jeff blocked the number, dialed, and handed it to Phil.

"Mercedes? Is this Mercedes Brooks?" Phil grinned and gave Jeff a thumbs-up.

"Johnny D'Amato. Long time, no see."

"Your mom gave me the number," he said, twisting the phone cord.

"No, I'm still living in—" Phil threw a pen at Jeff, who scribbled *L.A.* on the message pad.

"—California."

"I'm in town for the day. Just wanted to hook up."

"Not anymore. We just drifted apart. I thought I loved her, but then one day I woke up and looked at her, and knew I was a different man."

Oh, God, this is going to take forever. Jeff hammered on the paper with his pen.

"Sorry, I'm traveling with my boss, and he's a total nutcase."

Jeff cleared his throat.

"When, where can I meet you?" Phil asked, doing a great imitation of a guy on the make.

"You have plans? A date?"

"Oh, a friend. Well maybe I can meet up with the two of you. I'm not talking about moving in, and I don't want to change your life, but there's a warm wind—"

Jeff clapped a hand over Phil's mouth. "Don't blow this," he warned.

Phil glared. "Sorry. Bad connection. Tell me where you'll be and when. We'll meet up."

"Great. Can't wait."

"Too long."

Phil closed the phone with a snap. "Ten o'clock at Ecstasy."

Jeff took back his phone and chunked Phil on the shoulder. "Good job."

"You know, we should go for coffee some time."

Jeff looked at him evenly. "No."

"I had to try."

"I'll give you a raise."

Phil smiled happily. "You're the best."

MERCEDES AND SHELDON WERE CAMPED out at Ecstasy, one of the hottest meatmarkets in Manhattan's Meat-packing District. Not only had Sheldon got them into the upstairs VIP room, but she'd brought along her own mini-entourage of eye candy.

Brief introductions were performed. There was Carlos, with slicked-back dark hair and an unbuttoned white shirt that exposed rippling abs. Carlos, to no one's surprise, was a model.

Also there was Tommy, who wore khaki pants, a

Tommy Hilfiger button-down, loafers and no socks, which was so last decade, but Tommy's dad owned most of the ports in New York and Jersey, so bad fashion sense could be overlooked.

There was Enrique, who was another underwear model, and Christian, who had only one name and a thing for tight black leather that creaked when he walked, and then there was Davin, who was the group's token suck-up. Every time Sheldon spoke, he hung onto her every word, as if she was some rich knockout with a perfect body and perfect teeth. Okay, she was all that, but Mercedes didn't hold it against him. Besides, she was having too much fun.

The VIP room was everything that Mercedes imagined. It was wall-to-wall people with a customer-to-waiter ratio of three to one. There were martini glasses in blue with tiny yellow balls around the base. Very cute. And the ceiling was made of marble, not the rock marble, but the toy marbles. All shapes and sizes, some hanging low on string, some glued right to the top. The whole look was very textured, very fun.

Mercedes approved.

However, all fun aside, she was here on assignment, and it was time for her and Sheldon to get to work.

She scooted next to Sheldon, moving Davin out of the way.

"Excuse me," she told him with an innocent smile. "Can you get me a drink, please? Something with a lot of fruit in it. Fruit's very good for you."

He rose, with an unhappy look in those greedy eyes of his, and went to the bar.

Mercedes bumped Sheldon on the shoulder.

"You're going to have to help me with this one."

"You did okay all by yourself," said Sheldon.

"Let me set up the scene for you. Hot, happening club. Five studly men, all eager to do your bidding."

Sheldon's pink-tinted mouth drew up with disgust. "I don't do orgies."

"What are you willing to do for my brother?"

"Uh, no."

"You miss him?"

"Not in a mentally well-adjusted way."

Mercedes shot her a look of sympathy. "I'm sorry."

Sheldon pushed a hand through her hair and sighed. "I thought it'd be different. I thought we were different."

"Jeff is a man. Ergo, he is not different."

"You don't understand."

"I understand men," said Mercedes, "in the face of commitment, they run. Why's this any different?"

"We were friends. Sorta."

"Friendship between a man and a woman is impossible. Face it. Sex always becomes an issue."

"I don't have friends that don't want anything from me. Either money, or cachet, or a photo op. Jeff didn't want anything."

At that moment, Mercedes wouldn't have switched places with Sheldon for anything in the world. "You've proven my point nicely," she said, trying to joke, anything to inject some humor into the conversation. One fact she had learned from having two older brothers, one good punch line could heal a bruise faster than two million heart-to-heart talks. Heart-to-hearts weren't in her genetic makeup.

Sheldon gazed off into space, staring somewhere far beyond the room. "What am I supposed to do?"

"Let's start with something small and manageable, and then move on to bigger things. Let's get Jeff his job back. Close proximity will work wonders for the relationship, so tonight you'll have to go lower than you've ever gone before. Remember, we have to make Jeff look like the ultimate PR man by making you behave even worse without him. It won't be pretty. It won't be easy."

Finally, Sheldon cracked a smile. "You're a slave driver, Mercedes."

Mercedes nodded. "I know. Okay, so we have Enrique. You need to have him on the dance floor, and Christian, too. Tan, pale. It's a nice contrast, kind of like in a Madonna video. Have Christian behind, Enrique in front, and you will be the goddess letting them pleasure you."

"How are you going to write this up?"

"Enrique's bulgy bulges pressing against your womanly softness, Christian caressing the soft curves of your ass."

"I don't think Enrique has bulgy bulges."

"Hello? Fiction."

"Okay. That works." Then she got a worried look on her face. "Are you sure this will do it?"

"Of course. My plans are always successful. Now get out there, and do your duty for woman kind. I want every female in the place hating your guts."

Sheldon rose and whispered to Enrique and Christian, crooking a finger in their direction, flicking her long hair away from her face. Oh, she was good. Mercedes could learn from her, and the fact that she was willing to admit it said a lot.

Soon Sheldon was out on the dance floor, Christian plastered to her behind, Enrique nibbling on her neck, and the three of them looked as happy as a clam sandwich.

Mercedes pulled out her notebook and began to write.

Everything was going along fine until a shadow fell over the paper. She looked up, prepared to yell at whoever was blocking her light.

10

"WHAT THE HELL DO YOU THINK you're doing?" Jeff shouted much louder than necessary, but he didn't care. When Mercedes had screwed with Andrew's life, well, that was okay, but he wasn't going to let her screw with Sheldon's life, because Sheldon didn't need any help in that department.

He leaned low, specifically so that Mercedes could see the murder in his eyes. "You've gone too far this time, Mercedes. Don't mess with Sheldon, do you understand?"

"What are you talking about?" Mercedes flashed her Miss Innocent eyes in his direction, but Jeff knew exactly what his sister was doing.

"Can it, Mercedes. No more, do you understand?"

Mercedes looked behind Jeff, staring in the distance, a smile playing around her mouth. "Whatever you say."

Then she looked at him, and he could read that expression in her big brown eyes. It was the same look she'd got when he'd landed on Boardwalk, where she had just happened to own three hotels. It was the same look she had got when Mom had discovered that he'd smuggled Anne Levine into his bedroom after school. The list could go one. Jeff hated that look.

"What?" he asked.

She shrugged, a gesture implying many things, none of them good.

Slowly, he turned, and immediately saw her. Of course, it wasn't hard to notice the woman who was surgically attached to two dancing males.

Something ripped inside of him, and he wanted to look away, but he couldn't. He could only stare and hurt like hell. God, he'd been stupid—and played.

She looked up, saw him, and the vacant blue expression disappeared. Pain appeared in its place, but the vacant look returned soon enough, and she continued to gyrate, pulsate and vibrate, and Jeff felt the need to break something in two.

Eventually, he realized that he was standing there like a fool, and he wasn't doing anybody any good, so he turned to go. He had made it to the door, seriously wanting fresh air, when he felt a hand on his arm.

There were scarlet-tipped nails touching him, fingers that made him lose all bits of self-control, fingers that would slowly pull him into hell.

He took a deep breath and shook off the hand. "What do you want?" he asked, staring at a point over her head.

Sheldon didn't answer, so he lowered his gaze. She looked so worn, so beaten, so lost. "I didn't want you to leave."

"I think you've got enough company for tonight."

"It's not what you think, Jeff."

He wanted to believe her, wanted to think that there was some innocent explanation for two guys groping her like ripe produce on the dance floor, but he, the king of spin, couldn't come up with anything good enough. "What is it then, Sheldon? Covering for your sister again?"

"No," she answered, which wasn't an explanation at all.

"You want to explain?"

"I'm doing this for you."

He laughed. "Sorry, I'm not into that sort of thing."

She reached out again and touched him. This time he didn't shake the touch away. It felt too good. "Jeff."

"What do you want from me, Sheldon? You're not my job anymore."

"That's all it was?" she said, choking on the words. "A job to you? The night on the beach? Was that a part of the job, Jeff?"

"You're almost engaged," he said, reminding her, reminding him.

"You didn't answer my question."

It was the smile that kicked him in the gut. He backed her up against the wall until he felt the beat of her heart through his skin. He ground his hips against her, making sure she felt his hard-on, because it didn't matter who she danced with or slept with, he still wanted her.

Her fingers cupped his jaw and she kissed him. He didn't want to kiss her back, she didn't deserve it. But he couldn't help himself. Once he felt the soft, warm mouth on his, everything came pouring out.

He kissed her, his tongue tangling inside her mouth, his body absorbing hers, reveling in the curves, the softness, the toxic scent of her. It'd only been three days, but it felt like three years. His hands swept down her breasts, the turn of her waist, the curve of her ass, and everything felt exactly as he remembered in his dreams.

Jeff was oblivious to it all until he felt an elbow in his back, and his mind registered exactly where they were. No.

This was Sheldon's way, not his. He wouldn't be a spectacle, didn't like the spotlight, that was for her.

He lifted his head, removed his hands, and worked to breathe again. "See ya, Sheldon," he said, giving her a careless wink.

And carefully he walked, one step in front of the other, until he made it safely through the door.

SHELDON STAYED PLASTERED AGAINST the wall until her knees began to work again. There were times when she truly hated Jeff, when she hated his I-don't-give-a-damn attitude, when she hated the way he zoomed nonstop through life.

And she wanted to hate him now. She truly did. But parts of her were not cooperating, not cooperating at all.

She closed her eyes, cleared her head and walked back to where Mercedes was sitting.

"You have enough to write?"

Mercedes looked at her closely. "Are you okay?"

Sheldon pulled up her vintage why-should-I-give-a-flying-flip look and cocked her head. "Of course."

"Why do you do it?" asked Mercedes.

"Do what?"

"Never mind." Mercedes took a sip of her drink and stood. "We can go if you want."

"That'd be great. I have a killer headache."

"I bet," answered Mercedes.

Sheldon kept her eyes straight ahead. She was a little too naked right now, and she wanted to go home and hide.

"You're still going to do this?" asked Mercedes, as they walked outside the club, crowds parting in Sheldon's wake.

"Do what?"

"Help Jeff."

Sheldon thought long and hard, tempted, so tempted to say no, but she couldn't. Deep inside her, she wanted him to look at her with respect again, with gratitude even, those dreamy brown eyes seeing her for who she could be.

Maybe someday.

Maybe never.

"Yeah, I'm still in."

Mercedes bumped her fist. "That's my girl. Remember, the worst is yet to come."

MERCEDES WAS RIGHT. The next morning, Sheldon drank her latte while reading the latest character annihilation of her in *The Red Choo Diaries*.

Nine hours ago at Ecstasy, it wasn't just the neon that was getting lit up. In the VIP room, the action got hot and hotter still when one platinum-blond bombshell took on not one, but two hunka-hunka-hunks, and burned up the dance floor in a manwich sandwich. Reliable sources at the scene had the heiress entertaining a ménage a twat at her private table where things began to really get serious. The temptress sat in the lap of her Latin Lover, her skirts charmingly flared, while we all knew what was transpiring underneath. If our torrid imaginations weren't "steaming up the windows" enough, the Meg Ryan impersonation she performed—back arched in ecstasy, frenzied cries of "yes, yes"—drew raised eyebrows and one or two camera phone shots, which were immediately confiscated.

Sheldon shut off the computer, having read enough. Gossip had never bothered her in the past, but even she'd a line in the sand that she wouldn't cross, and two men at the same time, however interesting logistically, wasn't her scene. Of course, the noble gesture she was making would be much easier if Jeff could appreciate what she was doing for him and swear undying gratitude, among other things.

If last night was any indication, undying gratitude was rather moot at this point. Polite gratitude was pretty much out of the question; in fact, everything except for a toe-tingling mouth-mauling was pretty much all she was going to get.

Damn.

She rubbed her lips, still able to taste him there. Sheldon got up and poured her coffee down the drain—no point dwelling on life's injustices. After all, in most people's eyes, she had it all, she should be jumping up and down for joy and drinking champagne out of her slippers. Before she could contain the bubble of happiness that she was supposed to be feeling, the buzzer rang and Sheldon answered.

It was Cami.

"What are you doing here? I thought you'd be studying or something," said Sheldon.

"I wanted to say thanks," said Cami, settling down on the couch. Which meant she was going to be there for a while.

"Oh, gee, you're welcome," said Sheldon, sitting down across from her, cuddling a throw pillow in her lap.

"You didn't have to do it."

"Well, Mom would have had a heart attack and died at an early age, and I didn't want that."

"Sheldon?"

"What?" asked Sheldon, deciding that, okay, she could forgive her sister for having fun, falling in love and, in general, having a great life.

"I think I want to get married. To Lance. He asked me last night."

Sheldon struggled for air. "Don't you think this is a little sudden?"

"Well, no, how long does it take to know that I can't wait until the next time I see him, or that I reach out sometimes to touch him just because I want to make sure he's not a dream, or when he holds me—"

"Stop there. TMI." Cami looked so happy, so peaceful, so content. Meanwhile, Sheldon wanted to throw a pillow at her. "Do you want something to drink?" she asked, because she wasn't a pillow-thrower and wouldn't Cami understand the emotional cartwheels that Sheldon was currently dealing with?

"Do you have champagne?"

"In my apartment? No?"

"Sheldon, you're supposed to be this party girl. You need champagne."

"I'll have some delivered tomorrow. Why champagne?"

Cami stretched out on the couch, her feet dangling over the end. "Because we need to celebrate. We're both getting married to two marvelous men."

Sheldon got up to pour her sister a glass of water. "I don't think we should celebrate your getting married yet."

"We've been talking. We can fly to the islands and have a ceremony on the beach, like what I told you. I know, we can have a joint ceremony."

Sheldon sat down and realized that one sister needed to be the voice of reason, and right now she was the only one left. "Cami, could he be marrying you for your money?"

"I'm sure that's part of it, but not all. I mean, he likes to be with me."

"But doesn't that bother you? That if you were poor, he wouldn't be interested?"

"I think he'd be interested. Though I don't think he'd have proposed after two months of dating. I mean, I'm a really good catch, you know?" Cami pushed back the hair from her eyes in a gesture that their mother used all the time.

"And you're okay with that?" asked Sheldon, trying to wrap her mind around the idea that having loads of cash was the equivalent of a C-cup size, or a pouty, bee-stung mouth or any other of a million intangibles that made a female more attractive to the male sex.

"You deal," said Cami, summing it all up in two words. "I mean, your getting married is a business merger. Josh is a nice guy and all, but do you think you'd be marrying him if not for Toothbrite toothpaste?"

It took a minute for Sheldon to catch on that Cami expected an answer. "I don't know," she replied, which sounded better than an absolute no.

"And speaking of Josh, has he seen all the trash they've been writing about you?"

"I don't know. He hasn't said anything," said Sheldon vaguely.

"I can't believe the lies they print. Two guys! Imagine! I mean, imagine! You didn't do it, did you?"

"No, I was there, but we were just dancing."

"Two guys?" Cami gave her a thumbs-up. "That's pretty awesome, sis." And then it was enough about Sheldon and back to Cami. "So, what do you think Mom will say about Lance?"

"After the heart attack? I don't know, Cami. Mom and Dad have these visuals of what we're supposed to be, and I'm not sure they like having reality crash into their happy world."

"Jeez, Sheldon, when did you get to be so bitter?"

Sheldon bit her lip. "I'm not bitter, I'm worldly. There's a difference."

"I think that was bitter."

"Shut up, Cami."

"All right, so you think Mom and Dad'll have issues about Lance and me getting married?"

"Doubt it. Even with the tattoos and the band thing, they'll let you do whatever they think will make you happy." Mom and Dad would do whatever would make Sheldon happy, too. But all the money in the world couldn't make Jeff fall in love with her.

Cami smiled easily. "That's what I thought, too." Then she popped up, full up life and optimistic energy, and came over to give Sheldon a hug. "You're the best."

After she left, Sheldon just sat looking out over the big glass view of Central Park. She watched the dots, or rather, the people moving along the sidewalk. Each dot represented someone who was living their own life, dealing with disappointments and failures on a daily basis. But Sheldon had a perfect life. She'd brought up in a world where failures didn't exist, disappointments were whited-out, and mistakes were covered up with an abundance of cash.

THE SHAKE-OFF AT ROCKEFELLER CENTER was underway when Andrew arrived. Jeff pulled his ThinLife hat low and pretended that he didn't see his brother. Andrew instantly saw through the ploy and came over.

"So, who's the favorite?" Andrew asked, nodding toward the center court where five very nice ladies had come from all parts of the United States in order to share their delicious diet shake recipes.

Jeff crossed his arms over his chest. "I don't play favorites," he said, even though the schoolteacher from Oregon had his vote. She was nice, had a very photogenic smile, and her chocolate-raspberry shake recipe kept ThinLife from tasting like mud. A big plus in Jeff's mind.

"How much longer?"

"The judges are finishing up now."

"You're better than this, Jeff."

"Don't start, Andrew," said Jeff, his eyes hidden behind dark sunglasses.

"Weinberger called. He'd love to talk to you." Andrew snapped his fingers. "I could have you out of this. Doing car campaigns, or brands for international conglomerates."

"I like this," said Jeff through gritted teeth.

Andrew sighed. "I'm trying to help. That's all."

"I don't need your help."

"Uh, I think you do. I know what happened with Sheldon."

~~Jeff whipped off the sunglasses. "What do you mean?"~~

"I know her escapade documented in *The Diaries* is what got you fired from the account."

Jeff realized that Andrew didn't know everything, and he wasn't going to correct any misassumptions. "So what?"

"Can you please stop with the bullshit for once?"

"It's my job."

"Fine."

"Fine."

"Are you okay?"

"I'm fine. Tell me why you're here."

Andrew looked around furtively, and by nature, Andrew wasn't a furtive person. Jeff was intrigued.

"I need to go shopping."

"I know that, moron."

Andrew hedged for a minute. "For a ring."

"Holy cow!" Jeff slapped his brother on the arm. "Congratulations. You are such a fool."

Andrew got a stubborn look in his eyes. "Jamie's wonderful."

Before Jeff could say more, the crowd erupted into applause and cameras began to flash. Sure enough, the Oregon schoolteacher had won. Jeff smiled politely and offered her a handshake. She threw himself at him and began to cry joyful tears.

Jeff put the sunglasses back on and let her cry. Several moments passed before the tears dried up and she took his hand, pumping it up and down. "I can't believe I won."

"You had the best recipe," he told her earnestly,

keeping his voice quiet enough that Andrew couldn't hear his opinion.

It wasn't soon enough before the crowd began to disperse and Jeff was free once again. He looked over at Andrew, still not grasping this new tilt in the universe. "I can't believe this."

"Why?"

"I don't know. I didn't think you'd ever get married."

"I didn't either," admitted Andrew, as they began to walk toward Fifth Avenue.

"So why're you going to do it?"

"I love her."

"But there're so many women in the world. Don't you ever think you'd disappoint them if you tied yourself to one female?"

"No. When you meet the right woman, you don't want anybody else."

Jeff blocked out that last part. Over the past few months, he hadn't flirted with, kissed or nailed any other woman but one, and nobody was going to label her the right woman, only the wrong one. "But how do you *actually* know you don't want anybody else? I mean, you could want somebody else, but your brain doesn't pick up on it because there's so much interference, so you miss it. What if you're together for like, I don't know, four months, and you don't want anybody else, but what if, in month five, you wake up, your brain is clear and decides you do want somebody else?"

"It doesn't work that way."

"It could."

"Martians could come down and land on the Empire State Building, too."

Jeff looked up at the sky. "Not as likely."

Andrew sighed, sticking his hands in his pockets as they nudged past the pretzel vendor and the crowds hitting Saks. "I just know. I want to grow old with her. I want to work crossword puzzles with her. I want to argue with her, and I want to make up with her."

"You are so whipped."

Andrew nodded. "Yup." Then he grinned, arrogant and cocky. "But so is she."

"And that's why it works?"

Andrew nodded and stopped. "We're here."

Jeff looked up, at the discreet gold sign. "Tiffany's?"

"Well, yeah, it was either here or Harry Winston, and deep down inside, Jamie's an old-fashioned girl."

"It'll cost you a fortune!" exclaimed Jeff, realizing the full extent of his brother's illness.

"I don't need an excuse to spend my money."

Jeff felt faint. "This is what love does to you?"

Andrew shrugged. "Someday you'll know."

"I swear, and as God is my witness, I will never be this stupid. Never."

His brother only smiled.

11

ON FRIDAY MORNING, JEFF SAW Phil's sorrowful glance, and forced a smile. "Morning, Phil."

"It's not a good one, boss."

"Rule number one, Phil. I don't want to hear about your personal life."

"My personal life is fine. *The Red Choo* has struck again. I don't know why they want to ruin so many innocent people's lives, flushing them away like flotsam."

"Okay, Phil, I'll just be heading into my office now."

"You don't need to run away, boss. If you ever need someone to talk to—" Phil put a hand on his heart "—I'm here."

Jeff ran and shut the door to his office, flipped on the computer and zoomed over to see what smut Mercedes had chosen to post today.

Poor little rich girl, out partying late last night at Bar Nine with a full entourage of male models in tow. *Très* Madonna. After demonstrating to the crowd one hundred and one creative uses for a champagne bottle, she was taken out by "her boys" for who knows what sort of sexualicious activities. We can only imagine what as partaken of, and if someone wants to write in with a report, well, then we don't have to imagine anymore.

Jeff sighed, started to dial Mercedes and then decided there would be no point. He picked up the concept sheet for the next ThinLife commercial, but had trouble concentrating on the words in front of him.

Eventually, he put the document down because his mind was occupied elsewhere. Why was Sheldon doing this? It didn't make sense, and although he never thought she was a firm believer in the whole idea of rational thinking, it occurred to him that she must be up to something.

But what? Rumor had it that in the four days since Jeff's firm was let go, Wayne Summerville had already fired two other PR agencies, and although New York had lots to choose from, frankly, Wayne would be running out of choices soon.

No, there was some incomprehensible idea running around in Sheldon's head, and Mercedes, damn her poison pen, was participating in the plot. Jeff took a last look at the concept sheet, checked his watch and realized that it was Friday, nearly lunchtime. Maybe it was time for a little action, to see what Sheldon was up to, discover who "Stefan" was, and find out why she needed to wear a disguise.

Jeff picked up a ThinLife baseball cap, jammed it on his head, put on his sunglasses, took off his tie and untucked his shirt, and voilà, another typical New York slacker dude, albeit in a ThinLife baseball cap.

Jeff opened the door. "Phil, what other gimme caps do we have out here?"

Phil dug into his drawer. "I have Ford, Porsche, Bayer and Avon."

"Give me the Porsche hat."

"Sure." Phil shot him a look. "You trying to hide something?"

"No," Jeff replied. "Just going to lunch."

"Whatever you say, boss."

JEFF TOOK THE BROADWAY LINE to the Upper West Side where he had met Sheldon before. When his watch said it was eleven-thirty, he found a seat in the Starbucks across the street from the mysterious apartment building, and sat to wait it out. Two bottled waters later, surprise, surprise, she showed. Again, with the black wig.

She carried a Saks bag, big and bulky, just like before, too. Jeff left the Starbucks, but held back until Sheldon entered the building. He lagged behind, watching as she spoke to the doorman and was buzzed upstairs. Then Jeff fished in his wallet for some cash and approached the doorman, a fifty in his palm.

"Excuse me, sir. That lady who went up, I think she dropped this on the sidewalk outside."

The doorman held out his hand.

Jeff glared over his sunglasses. "If you don't mind, I'd feel better if I handed it to her myself. You tell me where she went, I'll take it upstairs and ask her. Thought if it's not hers, it would make a nice tip for your trouble."

The doorman pondered. "All right. She went to 23C."

Jeff smiled. "You're a good man—" he glanced at the doorman's nametag "—Nick."

When Jeff got to 23C, he stood at the door, hesitating, not sure if he wanted to ring the bell, not sure if he wanted to know exactly what was going on behind the door.

It all came down to whether he trusted Sheldon or not. If he trusted her, he could assume that whatever was going on behind that door was not sexual in nature. If he didn't trust her, well, all bets were off.

In the end, he raised his hand, and was about to push the button when the sounds from the apartment surprised him.

Music.

Strains of live music. Classical music.

Jeff hesitated again, thinking that maybe he was wrong to trust her, and that the haunting melody was some sort of mood music, but then the music stopped and a voice spoke up.

"No, that is wrong. You are too slow, and there is no passion in your playing. Give me a full bow, Sarah. From the second movement, and this time we'll do it right!"

Sarah? What the hell? There was no way that Sheldon was in that apartment with music students. No way at all.

No way at all...

Right?

A memory tickled the back of his brain. Jeff drummed his fingers on his arm for a moment, and then parked himself against the far wall in the hallway. Better to know for sure.

AT THE END OF THE LESSON, Sheldon packed up her violin and said her goodbyes. She had made it to the elevator doors when her body came alive, a tingling of the skin, the tangy scent of Hugo Boss cologne and a vague tightening of her nipples.

There was only one explanation.

Jeff.

Sheldon turned casually, as if she were studying the flocked wallpaper, and there he stood, leaning against the wall, arms crossed over his chest.

Stefan's apartment emptied out, and the other students joined her at the elevator. Sheldon took a step back, away from the group; she had a secret identity to protect.

"Do I know you?" she asked, hoping that he hadn't seen through her disguise.

"Shopping?" he asked, with a quirked eyebrow that eliminated any possible hope that he hadn't see through her disguise.

"Yes," she said, pasting a vacant smile on her face. The elevator arrived and the rest of the students got in. Sheldon started forward, but strong, stubborn fingers held her back.

Sadly, she watched the elevator doors close.

"What'd you get?" he asked, pointing at the Saks bag.

"Clothes," she answered.

"Can I see?"

"Nothing special."

"Then you won't mind," he said, taking the bag away from her.

"It's private," she said, resenting this unannounced invasion.

Jeff pulled out the case. "Most people wouldn't consider a violin private."

"There could be drugs in there," she stated defensively.

He opened it up. "Nope, just a violin."

"You don't know, they could be ground up in the polish used on the wood—"

"Sheldon, stop it. You're the only person I know who would rather be known as a drug runner than a music student."

And he had her. He knew it. She knew it, and it was time to let go. "All right. I'm taking lessons. I even told you once," she reminded him in case he forgot. "You didn't believe me."

His face got slightly flustered. "There was a certain inflection in your voice that indicated sarcasm. I went with the inflection. Sue me. Why the big disguise?" he asked, taking the wig off her head.

Sheldon automatically smoothed down her hair, because she always got a bad poof in the back from the wig, and she hated it. "It doesn't suit my image."

He threw his head back and laughed. "You are kidding me. No, I bet you're not." He packed her violin in the case, returned it to the bag, and took it from her. "Come on," he said. "I think we need to talk."

SHELDON MADE HIM GO TO HER apartment because she didn't like lugging the violin around the city. When they got inside, he looked around. "Very nice," he offered, sitting down on her couch.

It was a big couch, really, with room for four, but Sheldon went with the chair. It seemed smart.

"It's not as modern as yours," she said, because she'd rather talk about real estate than the violin, or him, or how he was doing, or if he was still mad at her.

"But the view is better here, and you have a lot more

square footage," he said, obviously going with the real estate dodge, too.

"I like the river. At first, I wasn't sure if the city scape would be nice. You know, the traffic, noise—"

Jeff held up a hand. "What're you doing, Sheldon? The truth."

Sheldon chewed on her lip momentarily, pondering how much she wanted Jeff to know about her. It wasn't easy. Nobody knew who she was, and she liked that. She sat alone in her own space, the golden tower her parents had set up for her long ago. But he had become a part of her tower, and she liked that, too. But he wasn't going to stay a part of the tower, and she didn't like that very much, but she understood there wasn't anything she could do to fix that. So…

"I don't know," she answered, not quite a lie, not quite the truth.

"Okay, let's do this the easy way. You've been hanging out with Mercedes, right?"

"Yes."

"And Mercedes has been writing things about you that aren't very flattering."

"Yes."

"And you're okay with that?"

"Yes," answered Sheldon honestly, because she could play this game.

"Why?"

Another hard one. "Because Mercedes had a plan," Sheldon answered vaguely.

"A plan that concerned…?"

Sheldon glanced around the room, pursing her lips. "Columbia-Starr Communications."

That surprised him, she could see it in his face. "My firm?"

Sheldon nodded.

She knew when it all clicked in his head—his eyes got bigger and he shook his head once. "You're doing this to get Columbia-Starr rehired."

Sheldon grinned and nodded.

"That is the stupidest plan I have ever heard. This was all Mercedes, wasn't it? You know, sometimes I think she's got something going on upstairs, and then boom—" He stopped in mid-rant. "But it's very nice of you to try."

Sheldon felt a warm flush in her face. "Thank you."

"Is it working?"

Sheldon hedged on that one because she knew she was close. Her father was inches away from the breaking point—that he was so near to popping that he'd agree to anything. "Kinda."

"Okay, so now I understand the whole manwich thing—" he ran a hand through his hair "—and I don't like it, but I understand it."

"I couldn't not do anything."

He sighed, and there was something in his eyes. Gratitude, maybe something more, or maybe it was her own wishful thinking, but the gratitude was *definitely* there and she was pleased.

"How long have you been taking violin lessons?"

"Six years."

"Does anybody else know?"

"No."

"Not even your sister, your mom?" he asked, watching her carefully.

"No."

"Again with the twenty questions?"

"It's easier that way," she told him.

"Fine. I'll pretend you're a focus group. Question number one: Do you think that most people believe that playing the violin is a bad thing or a good thing?"

"Good thing."

"Question number two: True or false, you do not want to be associated with playing the violin."

"True."

"Now we come to the why part of the program. Why do you not want people to associate you with playing the violin, which is a good thing?"

She hedged. "Because it's a good thing."

He banged the back of his head against the couch. "Okay, so you don't want people to associate good things with you?"

"Exactly."

"Why is this such a problem, Sheldon? And you know the answer to this question, just admit it."

"I'm a bad person," she said simply.

"You don't believe that."

"Not really," she admitted.

"You don't want to marry Josh," he told her.

"That's not true," she shot back.

"If you won't admit it to yourself, at least admit it to me."

She gave him a look. "That doesn't even make sense."

"And you do? Come on, you've been dancing around, and over, and above, and below. Just admit it."

"Maybe," she answered. "And that's as far as I'm willing to go."

"Tell your father."

"Jeff, we've had this discussion before. I'm a schlub. I party, I shop. I contribute nothing to my life, nor my family, nor to society as a whole. I want to do this."

"But you don't," he answered back.

"But I do. I really do." Sheldon pushed her hair away from her face and tried to make him see. "Haven't you ever felt like you wanted to contribute something to your family?"

"All the time."

"And if you had the opportunity to do something that would benefit your family, even if it meant being inconvenienced, wouldn't you do it?"

"No."

"I don't believe it."

"Maybe I would, but not on the scale of marrying somebody as a token family gesture."

"It would be a big benefit to my family. Huge, life-changing. It's my dad's dream."

"What about you, Sheldon? What's your dream?"

Sheldon didn't like that question, it made her think of things that she never allowed herself to think about, but Jeff had a way of digging inside her that made it easier to face the truth. "You're going to laugh."

"I won't laugh. I told you I wanted a boat. I swear, I won't laugh."

"I want to play the violin."

"But you already do."

"In...Carnegie Hall."

He leaned forward, almost coming off the couch. "You're kidding," he said, a smile on his face.

"You said you wouldn't laugh," she reminded him.

"This isn't my laughing face. I'm just getting adjusted to the image, that's all."

"You think it's silly?" she asked nervously. Secretly, she thought it was silly, ludicrous, and the butt of many late-night comedians' jokes.

His face softened, and he knelt beside her chair. "Sheldon, I don't think it's silly at all. Why music?"

Sheldon considered her answer, trying to put it into the right words. "I always felt different from everyone else. I mean, we were brought up that way, so that's not a surprise, but I never connected with people." Until now, she thought to herself. He was watching her carefully, not laughing at her, not thinking she was a snob. Understanding.

"And music connects to you?"

She nodded. "Before, it was as if I was from some foreign planet and didn't know the language. But when I hear music, or when I play, it makes sense. It's real. That sounds stupid, doesn't it?"

"Music is beauty to the ear instead of the eye. You're just wired a little differently than most."

"Really?" she asked, not believing him, but wanting to believe him.

"Really. But actually…"

And there it goes. "What?"

"No, I shouldn't tell you."

"What?" she repeated.

"Nah, you wouldn't do it."

"What?" she snapped, ready to do bodily harm by this point.

"Before I decide if it's silly or not, I should hear you play."

"No," she answered flatly. "Not an option."

"Then how do I know if it's silly or not. What if you suck?"

"I don't suck," she told him, annoyed by the way he was looking at her, waiting for her to prove it to him. And she knew what he was doing, the sneaky devil, and it only ticked her off even more.

He held up his hands, palms up. "Just saying."

For a second, she wondered if she dared. Still, the way he looked at her with those eyes, she felt as if she could do anything. That was why she loved him. He made her believe that she, Miss Schlub Extraordinaire, could do anything, anything at all. Her mind rushed with the possibilities of a world that was opening up before her, all because she loved him.

The feeling washed over her, her numbed self coming alive. The tingles began, in her skin, in her mind, in her heart. Painful at first, but then the blood began to pump through her, warming her, and it was like music playing inside.

She stood on wobbly legs.

"You swear you won't laugh."

"Swear," he answered.

Sheldon picked up her case, pulled out the violin and took a deep breath. She could do it; she knew she could. She closed her eyes, lifted the violin to her shoulder, and began to play Handel's Sonata No. 3.

At first, it was excruciatingly painful, with a tortured screech in the third stanza. It would have been easier if she didn't care what he thought, but she did, and she wanted to do her best. However, then the music began to soothe her and she stopped wondering if he would think she was a spaz and focused on her finger shifts, the strokes of the bow, sounding her vibrato like Stefan had insisted she should. Before she knew it, she had gotten through the entire first movement, and, not wanting to put Jeff to sleep, Sheldon stopped, her eyes still closed.

When she heard him clapping, she peeked open one eye. When she saw the expression on his face, she opened the other eye, as well. "You liked it?"

He nodded. "You don't suck."

As great compliments in history go, it wasn't up there with anything Shakespearean, but her heart felt lighter, and the oxygen was thinner, and there was a lump in her throat that wouldn't go away.

Sheldon turned to look out the window because she didn't want him to see her eyes. The feelings in her were too new and too raw. Very precisely she put away her violin and then pretended a great interest in the view of the Hudson.

He came to stand behind her, not touching her, which somehow made it worse. "You should play in Carnegie Hall."

She stayed still, determined not to look at him. "I haven't been playing long enough. I'm too old to be really great."

Then his arms slipped around her like a warm blanket on the first night of winter. She tried not to lean into him, she didn't want to depend on him, but her body didn't listen.

His lips feathered against her neck. "I missed you," he said.

Thousands of words flew through her brain. Why

didn't you call? Did you lay awake at night, staring at the ceiling, wondering if I was alone? Exactly how much did you miss me?

Sheldon was silent. He shifted her in his arms, and then they were kissing, and everything she didn't say, she knew he could taste it on her lips.

It'd been less than a week, but this... This was like being home. She pulled him closer, arms wrapping around his waist, because he didn't know how much she needed him.

Sunlight burned down on them, and the kiss went on forever. She could stay here, wrapped in his arms, not moving, just drowning in him. This was different from the night on the beach, there was passion, but penance as well.

He raised his head. She lost herself there, wanting to believe in him, wanting to believe in her, and she gave him a shaky smile, probably not the sexiest move she'd ever made, but effective nonetheless.

Without a word, he pushed down her jeans, fumbling fingers lingering on the curve of her hip as he exposed it, and she knew she wasn't the only one with needs. It heated her like the sunbeams touching her skin. He slipped a hand between her thighs, grinding against her, and the heat burst into flame. Her breathing grew shallow and she couldn't stand, not anymore.

His free hand slipped behind her, guiding them to the couch, easing her down. She pulled her shirt over her head, and he stood for a moment above her, watching. The darkness in his eyes was backlit with desire, and it captivated her, her mind dazzled with the possibilities of now.

"Your turn," she said, trying to be flippant and sophisticated, but it was more of a throaty whisper, because he made it so hard to talk, to think, to breathe. Thankfully, he didn't seem to notice and complied with her request. He quickly tossed off shirt, pants, boxers and she sighed at the sight of him. No boy there, all man. The sun lingered on him, a sailor's tan, she realized, and his shoulders were broader than she remembered. That was Jeff, long and lean, but unless you looked closely, you wouldn't see the strength. "You should be a model," she told him.

"No freaking way." He smiled and eased himself on top of her. The moment their bodies met, she came alive. Her nerves betrayed her. His mouth met hers, and she wanted to stay detached and uncaring, but his lips were so persuasive, coaxing her into a response that was anything but detached. She nipped at his lip, then traced it with her tongue, needing to hang onto her sanity, needing to hang onto her pride, but he was determined to make her lose it.

She put a hand over his chest, feeling the strong beat, feeling it match hers, and then she smiled inside, letting go.

Her hands, now unhampered by anything as unimportant as pride, skimmed the hardness of his thighs, the muscles in his back, his butt, tracing and memorizing, finding the outline of a scar, the dimple in his knee.

"You're making me nuts," he whispered against her neck, pulling her hands underneath him. She wasn't happy, because there was much more to explore, but then he pumped inside her in one thick, hard stroke.

She stopped mid-breath, assailed by a wave of pleasure, hazy, mindless pleasure. Then she began to ride the pleasure, began to ride him, playing him like her violin, hearing the music inside her. His music.

Again and again, he thrust inside, but this time she knew and was prepared. Her hips rose up to meet him, answering, and he pushed deeper inside her.

She pushed back.

He looked at her in surprise.

She gave him a slow smile. Really, when would he learn not to underestimate her?

And so they went, round and round. He would push, anticipating the fight. She took him, her thighs locked around his waist. She raked her nails down his chest, shimmying against him. He pressed her down into the cushions.

She ran her fingers along his back, and lower still, raising her eyebrows when he froze.

He took her hands and locked them above her head.

She nipped at the skin of his earlobe, his neck, his chest.

He took her breast in his mouth, and nipped back.

Okay, that stopped her for a minute. And in that minute, he took very serious advantage. He increased his pace, thrusting hard and fast, and she struggled to keep up, she wanted to keep up. For him this was always a battle against some demon she didn't understand. It was never just pleasure and she wanted just the pleasure. For her, for him.

But soon she couldn't think, could only feel his mindless passion, passion that seeped into her. The throbbing rhythm beat in her head, building and taking over, filling her. His strokes were too hard, too quick. She closed her eyes, letting him plunder her, her body splitting apart.

He pushed deep, deeper still, and his wicked mouth closed around her breast. He bit—hard, and she screamed, and he thrust again, once, twice, three times…

Her orgasm shook her, ecstasy was hers as he took one last stroke and collapsed on top of her.

They stayed there, breathing heavily, slick skin pressed together. Her muscles weren't functioning, she knew it. She couldn't move at the moment, and didn't think she could ever move again.

All she managed was a tap of her finger on his back, mainly to see if her finger could function better than the rest of her.

He opened one eye.

"Just testing for signs of life."

"You kill me, Sheldon."

"Excuse me, I think I was the victimized party here," she answered.

"Complaining?"

"I should."

"But you're not," he said, his head collapsing against her breast, male pride apparent in his voice.

"I should," she repeated.

He raised his head, looked at her face and then pressed a kiss to her lips. "You should," he answered. "I can't think sometimes, it's like my brain stutters. I like being here, with you, in you, talking to you."

"So what's bugging you?" *Why can't you love me,* she thought to herself.

"Nothing," he answered, his face closing off.

"Translation, you're not going to say."

"Maybe. Not yet."

Which wasn't a promise, but it was a start. She smiled against his hair, memorizing the scent. "We're going to have to move."

"Tomorrow."

And she thought that tomorrow would be fine, but then she felt his cock stiffen. She raised an eyebrow.

He looked at her apologetically. "I told you that I missed you."

"You think you could go a little easier this time?"

He thought for a minute. "I have an idea," he said, sliding down between her legs.

Immediately she knew what he was up to. "Oh, no," she half groaned, but his lips were nuzzling her stomach, lower, teasing the tops of her thighs, and the darkness began again.

His tongue teased inside her, and she leaned her head back deep into the pillows. "Do what you must," she told him, her body already beginning to shudder. Mentally, this couldn't be good for her brain, but merciful heaven, the rest of her was really, really, really happy.

12

JEFF HEARD THE BUZZING IN HIS pants, but ignored it.

"Your phone is ringing."

"Voice mail," he told her. Right now, there were more important things in life, like the curve of her ass. They had migrated from the living room, to the bedroom, and then back to the living room again. Currently he had her stomach down on the carpet, while he admired the color of the sunset on bare flesh.

It was a great shade of gold, and he wondered if a camera could ever capture that exact shade. Maybe a painter, but he didn't think so.

His pants stopped buzzing, and her telephone started up.

"It's Mercedes," said Sheldon, lifting her head, the blond hair slipping down her back.

"Who cares?" he asked, pressing a kiss against the back of her knee. She wore something on her skin and it tasted like peaches. A man could live on peaches forever.

"I was supposed to go out with her last night."

"So she can write some new slander about you?"

"Dad's really close to conceding to my demands."

"You've made demands?"

"Not really. That's not the way I work."

She rolled over, pillowing her head on her hands. He sucked in a breath, because she had no idea how the sight of her affected him. So casual, so careless, and he knew that one day she'd look at him, her blue eyes warm, her bare curves golden from the sun, and he'd stop breathing and wouldn't be able to start again.

For most of his life, Jeff had coped with his place in the cosmic universe. He wasn't the hot-shot trader that Andrew was, he didn't have Mercedes verve, he didn't have his mother's impossible dreams. He just wanted to exist, content with getting-by. He glided through life on a wink and smile, and giving women a good time. It wouldn't cure cancer, but it was all he had. He didn't want to dream beyond his reality, didn't want to imagine things that he wasn't capable of, he liked to stay happily contained within the four walls of his life. But there were times, dark, anxious times when he felt it within him—the restless urge to do more, be more, strive more, and then his more practical self would give him a punch on the arm and tell him to get over it. He wasn't, he couldn't, don't waste your time.

The restless urges were coming more and more often. With Sheldon, he wanted to be more. He wanted to be worthy, but he would never make it. So why try?

One word, one name, one woman.

Sheldon.

A pressurized balloon was filling up inside his chest, and he wanted to make a joke, something to prick it, relieve the pressure, but he couldn't think of one worthless thing.

"Jeff?"

He cleared his head. "So when's the wedding?"

She jerked back, her smile going cold. "The engagement's going to be announced in a couple of weeks." She stood up. "I think I'm going to take a shower."

He watched her walk, back stiff but still gorgeous, and he wished he wasn't such a jerk. Yet it was her fault for agreeing to the whole asinine idea. He followed her, intending to tell her exactly what he thought of the whole thing, but she had already stepped into the shower, water flowing over her. His hands flexed because he wanted to touch her again. So badly. For a second he merely watched, but then he turned around and went to the other room and dressed.

Why try? Why set himself up for failure? Before she got out of the shower, he was already gone.

WAYNE SUMMERVILLE CALLED HIM early on Saturday morning. "We're going to try this again, Jeff. Sheldon promised she'd fly right, less than two weeks to go, but there was a condition. She wanted Columbia-Starr back as her representation. I didn't think it was very smart, but she had her mind stuck on it, and so I told her okay."

"I'm not sure this is a good idea, Mr. Summerville," started Jeff, because he didn't think he could be around her.

"Now, now, don't tell me no, son. If it's money, rest easy. I'll make it worth your while."

"It's not the money, sir."

"Well, of course it's the money." Wayne lowered his voice. "I need your help here, and I need it bad."

Jeff closed his eyes. "All right," he said. "We try again."

"We're having a pre-engagement party on Sunday. Just the family. You should come."

Jeff rubbed his hand over his eyes. "Sorry, sir. I've got plans that night. You guys have a great time."

HE STARED AT THE PHONE ALL morning, knowing he was going to have to call her. But she beat him to it, she showed up at his apartment instead.

She was gorgeous as always, but there was a tired look in her eyes, and he hated that he'd put it there.

"Dad called?" she asked.

Jeff nodded. "Thank you."

"Anytime."

"Sheldon?"

"What?"

"I'm sorry. I shouldn't have said anything."

She flashed him a brittle smile. "Why not? Two weeks of freedom left, it's probably a good thing you reminded me."

"Can you stay for a minute?"

He thought she was going to say no, but then she nodded and curled up in one of his chairs.

"Call off the whole thing, Sheldon."

She gave him a searing look. "It's so easy for you to sit there and tell everyone else how to live their lives because it doesn't matter to you. They're someone else's feelings and someone else's responsibilities at stake. Not yours. I don't think you're in any position to tell me what to do, you know?"

"You're right," he answered softly. "I won't do it again."

"I'm going to a concert tonight at Lincoln Center."

"With Josh?" he asked, hating the edge in his voice.

"No."

"Do you want me to go with you?"

"Do you want to go with me?"

Jeff looked at her and saw the sadness in her eyes. He couldn't fix a lot of things, but he wasn't going to disappoint her again. "Yeah," he answered. "Boring music?"

She smiled halfway. It was a start. "Yeah."

"Oh, joy."

SHELDON DRESSED CAREFULLY THAT night. Discreet black, nothing overt like her usual style. Everything nicely covered, the butterfly going back in the cocoon. Tonight was the start of the rest of her life. Everyone had told her she had to grow up, and she finally realized that everyone was right.

She pulled her hair back in a bun, no little tendrils hanging, everything nicely and neatly in place.

She surveyed the results, decided she needed more blush because she looked dead, and after pinking her cheeks, she stood back, satisfied.

This was Sheldon Sumerville, soon to be fiancée of Joshua Conrad, soon to be part owner of Summerville-Con-Mason Consumer Products, one of the larger consumer products conglomerates in the world. She certainly looked the part.

Jeff would approve.

It was hell to be in love with a man who hid his heart even more completely than Sheldon did. It was easier to admit it to herself now. She loved him. He had caused this metamorphosis within her, a change she had never thought possible. He made her grow up. Made her look at the world with eyes wide open.

He expected things from her. The ironic thing was that he never expected anything from himself. That, she couldn't fix.

This morning she had gone to him, hoping he would come around, say something, anything. He wanted her to call the engagement off, but never because of him. Oh, no, Jeff was extra-specially careful to avoid any mention of a "them" or an "us." Always "her." Always solo.

Of course, she should be grateful for that reality check. He would sleep with her, make love to her, probably even care for her in his own way, but now it was time for Sheldon to contemplate her own future— a future just like she'd planned. So, for two more weeks, she was free and unattached, and she would take those two weeks, make enough memories to last a lifetime and then be on her way to her brand-new life.

She practiced her smile in the mirror, nearly getting it right. No one could tell that a part of her was dying, but then, no one had ever been able to read Sheldon.

Except for him.

Her buzzer rang. He was here.

She picked up her purse and opened the door.

JEFF, WHO WAS NEVER WITHOUT WORDS, found himself speechless. This wasn't the Sheldon he knew, this wasn't a Sheldon he even knew existed.

Her dress was black, long and demure, clinging to her curves, a subtle hint at the beauty beneath. He'd never noticed the high cheekbones, the aristocratic tilt to her eyes, the proud lift to her chin.

He blinked once and held out an arm. It seemed the

thing to do when suddenly finding himself escorting a queen.

A cab was downstairs waiting, and now he wished he'd hired a car, but it was too late for that. It was too late for a lot of things.

She climbed in the taxi as though it didn't matter, and they rode in silence to Lincoln Center. It was a hard, uncomfortable silence, because he didn't know what to say. He'd spent so much time telling her what she was doing wrong, that when she started doing everything right, he felt lost and useless.

Jeff had been to Lincoln Center a few times before, not a place he frequented as a rule, but in his line of work, anything went.

The hall was packed with the upper crust of the upper crust there for the debut of some violinist from somewhere. He didn't know where, didn't really care. As they walked to their seats, he found himself glancing her way, waiting to see the old Sheldon return, but this stranger stayed in her place.

The lights dimmed, the conductor raised his baton, and the music began. Jeff watched Sheldon more than the stage. Watched the way her fingers worked silently to the music, watched the discreet foot tapping underneath her chair, watched her lips curve in a serene smile, and he began to understand.

This was what she loved.

When the soloist began to play, she leaned forward in her seat, enthralled by the sound. Jeff had to admit the guy was good, but he thought Sheldon could be that good if she wanted.

When her hand lighted on the armrest between them,

he took shameless advantage and covered the dancing fingers with his own. She looked over, startled, but he pretended to watch the music, and the dancing fingers stilled, but he was able to touch her, know the vision was real, and they sat that way for the rest of the performance until he saw her home.

JEFF STAYED AT HER APARTMENT that night, exactly as she had planned. When he walked her up to her door, she asked him if he'd like a drink. He said yes, and they never had a drink. As soon as she closed the door, he took her in his arms. The wildness was gone tonight, there was no battle. Instead he made love to her quietly, because the war was over.

Her dress disappeared into a pool of black on the floor. His tux neatly folded over a chair in her bedroom. He didn't speak, she couldn't talk, because there was an air of sadness in her, in him, and she didn't want to cry. There was a sweetness to his lovemaking that night, tenderness and something else. He was cautious and slow in his touches, as if she were something fragile and breakable.

That night, the only thing fragile and breakable was her heart. Maybe he knew, maybe he guessed. She didn't know, and they didn't speak of it.

He slept curled against her, holding her, and it was the first time that they had spent the night together. It was an odd thing, but she liked the feel of him next to her. Liked the way the hair covering his chest tickled her back.

Late in the night, when the sun began to rise, she turned to him, and he made love to her again. All was quiet, the slow even breathing, the hum of the air conditioning, the faint buzz of the city awakening far below.

A beginning and an ending, all at the same time.

13

LATER THAT SAME MORNING, Jeff returned home. There were eight messages on his answering machine. Four from Mercedes and three from his mom.

"Jeff, this is your mother. We're having a dinner for Andrew and Jamie Sunday night. I bet you can guess why. And I've got a new agent. Don't tell Andrew, he'll be angry, but I'm very excited. I have an audition for a commercial next week. It's a campaign spot, and I'm supposed to be the concerned constituent. I think I can do that. Be here at seven."

Jeff erased them all. He really didn't want a family thing tonight. He really didn't want a people thing tonight.

He collapsed in a chair, deciding it was too early to drink. It was Sunday after all.

The next call was Mercedes. "Where were you?"

"I was busy," he answered.

"What's her name?" she asked taunting him as only a younger sister could.

"You don't know her."

"Hmm. Have you heard from Sheldon? She stood me up on Thursday and she hasn't been answering her phone since."

"I'm not her keeper."

"Funny. I thought you were."

"What do you want Mercedes?"

"You owe me a grand."

"For what?"

"Our bet. Andrew asked Jamie to marry him."

"Yeah," said Jeff.

"Don't sound so peppy. It's only a thousand dollars, and our brother's lifelong happiness is on the line."

"Hmm."

"Have you seen today's paper?"

"No."

"You have to look. Go get it. I'll wait."

"Mercedes…"

"Jeff. Go. I'm waiting."

Jeff picked up the paper from the counter. "Got it."

"Now, turn to the Op-Ed page."

He flipped through the pages. "Yeah."

"Do you see it? Big, bold letters. America Needs More Sex by Mercedes Brooks."

Jeff threw the paper down on the floor. "Do you have no shame?"

"It's a great essay. And besides, you helped me write it."

"Shoot me now."

"I think Mom will be happy."

"Andrew will kill you."

"No he won't. He's riding that cloud of happiness called true love."

"It'll pop soon enough."

"What is wrong with you?"

"I've got a headache, okay?"

"Too much to drink, huh? It's killing what brain cells you have left."

"I'll see you tonight, Mercedes," he snapped, then hung up. Probably rude of him, but he didn't care.

He looked at his watch. Noon. Good. He opened the bottle of Chivas and toasted himself.

HIS MOM HAD COOKED LASAGNA, he could smell it from outside her apartment. Normally, Jeff loved her lasagna, but sitting on top of five shots of Chivas, he wasn't sure he could stomach the dinner.

Thea opened her door and gave him a big hug. "And look who's here." She sniffed, and then slapped him on the chest. "Already drinking? Mark my words, Jeffrey Alan Brooks, you are going to die an early death from all the liquor."

Jeff just smiled and went into the place.

Mercedes was there, as were Andrew and Jamie. Jeff waved carelessly and collapsed into the nearest chair.

Andrew glared at him, the Brooks evil-eye. "What the hell's wrong with you?"

Mercedes dabbed a tissue at the corner of her eye. "He was rude to me this morning."

"I'm always rude to you," Jeff shot back.

Their mother interrupted. "This isn't the time for fighting. We're here to celebrate a happy occasion. My son is getting married." She lifted a bottle of champagne. "*We'll* have a toast—" she said, then glanced at Jeff "—not you."

Andrew opened the bottle and poured glasses all around. Thea recanted and Jeff was permitted to participate.

He lifted his glass to Andrew and Jamie.

"To many long, long, long, long, long years of happiness, and kids, and china patterns, and SUV's that contribute to global warming—"

"Here, here," said Mercedes, cutting him off.

Jeff drank his champagne and was eagerly awaiting another glass, but his mother cut him off—this time for real.

By the start of dinner, Jamie was the only one who wasn't mad at him. She even talked to him while they ate. "How's work coming along?"

"Really good," said Jeff.

"He's doing diet food," said Mercedes, mainly because she needed to undercut him in everything. Jeff shot her an evil look.

"Am not. Got back the Summerville account. Summerville-Mason-Pricks-U.S.A."

Mercedes perked right up. "You got it back? You didn't say a word. And you know who got that account back for you? Me, that's who. And do I get a thank-you? Uh, no."

"You dragged Sheldon's name through the mud."

"But you got your account back, what does it matter to you?" she asked, and he hated the knowing look in her eyes.

"Just leave me alone," he said.

"Well, I have some news, too," she said.

"Yeah, she told everyone in New York they should be having more sex."

Mercedes snarled at him and then smiled at Jamie nicely. "I'm going on *The Sam Porter Show* Tuesday night."

"Really?" said Thea. "I love his show."

"He's a prick," said Jeff.

"Yes, yes, he is," agreed Mercedes. "And I'm going to show him the error of his thinking."

"Good luck," said Jeff.

"He wanted to talk about Sheldon and the diaries—"

"Don't you dare," snapped Jeff.

"I told him I wouldn't," replied Mercedes.

"If you say one word, sister, I'll—"

"You could come with me. Not on the show, of course. But you know, help me out, give me media guidance, blah, blah, blah. *And* make sure I don't say anything about Sheldon. If you do, I'll waive the thousand bucks you owe me."

"You owe Mercedes a thousand dollars?" asked Andrew. "For what?"

"She bet you'd propose within a month. I said it'd take at least three."

Jamie started to laugh. Andrew didn't see the humor. The rest of the dinner went downhill from there.

SHELDON'S PRE-ENGAGEMENT PARTY was at her parents' condo on the Upper East Side. It wasn't her choice, but she didn't say anything. There wasn't a point. She'd bought a light blue dinner suit especially for the occasion. It made her think of Jackie O, and she liked that imagery.

"Cocktail wiener?" asked Cami, holding out a plate with a straight face.

"Certainly," said Sheldon, popping one in her mouth.

"Martini?" asked Cami, scooting Sheldon up to the bar where a handsome gentleman awaited her drink order.

"Certainly," said Sheldon, deciding that this would

be an evening best experienced through the comforting haze of alcohol.

"Make it a double," whispered Cami to the bartender. "How're you holding up?"

Sheldon nodded. "Okay."

"You look great. Love the blue. Makes your eyes shine. Josh looks nice tonight," she said, pointing to Sheldon's fiancé-to-be, who did look nice, and was trying so hard, bless his heart. "You should talk to him, I think."

Sheldon didn't want to talk to him. She'd have the rest of her life to talk to him. What did one night matter?

She spotted her dad approaching from across the room, a proud gleam in his eye. Quickly, Sheldon downed the martini.

"Sheldon! Look at you! I swear, my girl is all grown up now. Makes me want to burst out in my own rendition of 'Sunrise, Sunset.'"

"Not here, Dad."

"Darling, I was making a joke. You lost your sense of humor?"

She gave him a kiss on the cheek. "No."

He took her arm and steered her toward Josh. "Now, you two kids sit here and chat while the rest of us old farts are sitting down to some cigars and whiskey." He looked at Josh. "Unless you'd like to come, too?"

Josh seemed uncomfortable at the thought. "I'll stay here and talk to Sheldon."

Wayne winked. "Got that."

And he left Sheldon and Josh alone.

"You look nice tonight," Josh told her.

"You too," she answered. And he did. All decked out in a tuxedo, he should make a girl proud.

"I wanted to talk to you about a ring."

"Oh, we don't have to worry about that yet."

"Well, when we have the meeting on Friday, I think I should have it. It'll make it feel official. What do you like? Solitaire, pear-cut, emerald-cut? Or we could go buy it together?"

Sheldon took a deep breath. "I'll trust your judgment on this one."

"You're sure?"

"Positive."

"Hey, I wanted to say that I appreciate what you're doing for me."

"I beg your pardon?"

"I've been watching the papers. I know you had some wild oats to sow, I've had some, too, but now that we're at the wire… Anyway, I wanted to say that I'm glad you got it out of your system." Josh had nice blue eyes, and what they lacked in passion, they made up for in empathy.

"Did you?" asked Sheldon, curious about his remarks. She had to admit that she'd never thought about how this was affecting him. He always seemed so confident, so determined in what he was doing. "Is there somebody you care about?"

"Not really," he replied, looking carefully away from Sheldon.

"'Not really' isn't no," said Sheldon.

He looked at her then, the first-born son of a tycoon firmly back in control. "It's a no. I think I've known since I was a kid that I'd be the future of Con-Mason, and everything else was pushed aside."

"Including your life," said Sheldon drily.

"Yeah, including that. You understand."

She nodded. "Yeah."

"You're okay with this, right? I wouldn't let you do anything you weren't good with."

"Oh, I'm fine with it. It's kinda nice, really."

"Really?"

"Yeah. I love my dad. He's got these huge dreams, and I could never do anything before. Now I can."

"They're good people, huh?"

"The best," answered Sheldon.

"You won't regret this," answered Josh. He leaned into her and kissed her. It was a polite kiss, controlled, not taking anything for granted.

Sheldon kissed him back, deciding she needed to get the hang of this. It wasn't too bad. Really. And if she quit listening to her heart, it would have been nice.

JEFF LEFT HIS MOTHER'S APARTMENT and found himself accidentally on the Upper West Side. She'd had her pre-engagement party tonight, and he wondered how it went. Probably smashing, with Josh taking her arm and the two of them strolling around the room, laughing, and Josh would tell her a joke, and she'd laugh, flashing him her fabulous smile, and he'd tell her about his yacht and how they would sail around the world on their honeymoon.

He sagged against a building because he definitely didn't want to think about the honeymoon. A wedding was bad enough, but a honeymoon, another man, seeing her, pounding inside her.

Jeff bent over and puked his guts out.

He found a bench in the park where he could see the corner of her window. He knew it was her window, because he counted, and even drunk, he still knew it was hers.

The lights came on, and he wanted to go up and talk to her, see her, make love to her, but he wasn't sure she was alone. And wouldn't that be an awkward moment? Oh, yeah, Josh, I'm her lover. You don't mind, do you?

He only had five nights left with her, and the bastard had stolen one from him. For a few minutes, he let himself dream. If he were rich and powerful, like Andrew, for instance, he would have her. They would have a boat, double-masted, teak decks, and a cabin down below where he could hold her in his arms at night, and it would be his name on her lips. Not anyone else's.

It was a good dream. It was a great dream, actually, but Jeff knew a dream when he saw it. He would never be the hugely successful type. He was the slacker of the family. The one who'd chosen PR because it was easy. And fun. Didn't want to forget about the fun.

He stood up and wiped his mouth, and decided he wasn't ready to go home. No, this was New York, where, if a man couldn't get laid, then hell, he wasn't a man.

He found a bar on Fifty-seventh, off Sixth. It was a modern, expensive place with eighteen-dollar martinis and women who wore his annual salary in clothes. But Jeff wasn't worried about that. When it came to sex, class didn't matter. It was just two people having a good time.

He picked her out right away. She was a redhead, he couldn't do a blonde. Not yet, anyway.

He went to the bar by himself and ordered a soft drink. He'd already had too much, and sobriety was important in a seduction.

It didn't take long, she was there by his side in less

than two minutes. Women liked Jeff, they always had. He wasn't sure exactly what the appeal was, but he didn't complain either.

"What's your name?" he asked.

"Shelby," she answered, and he frowned, because he didn't like that name.

"What's your middle name?" he asked.

"Carol," she told him.

"Do you mind if I call you Carol? I like that better."

She leaned over and kissed his cheek. "Not a problem. You seem like you're in a bad mood. The moon is high, the drinks are cold and you've got a warm woman on a bar stool next to you. What's not to love?"

"I'm not in a bad mood."

She raised her eyebrows.

"All right. Can we not talk about my mood? Tell me about you instead. Are you having a nice night?"

Her hand crept up his thigh. "I'm having an amazing night, and I think it's only going to get better."

"Yeah, well, I don't think it could get any worse…"

"Why don't you take me back to your place? We'll make it all better."

Jeff looked at her, auburn hair, green eyes and a moist red mouth that was made for all sorts of good things. It wasn't a bad idea. It truly wasn't.

"Sure," he said. "Let's go."

14

Monday morning came way too early for Jeff. He wore his sunglasses into work and made a New Year's–type resolution to never drink Chivas again.

Actually, the way his head was pounding, he didn't think he wanted to drink alcohol ever again.

He tried to sneak past Phil's desk but no luck there.

"Oh… That looks ragged."

Jeff stared at him over the sunglasses. "Don't we pay you to work?"

"I call 'em as I see 'em, boss. Aspirin?" he asked, holding up the bottle and shaking it.

Jeff took the bottle and stuffed it in his pocket. "I'll be in my office. See that I'm not disturbed."

"Sleep will do wonders," whispered Phil.

Actually, he never got to sleep. Ten minutes later, Phil buzzed. "Wayne Summerville is here."

"Oh, goody. Send him in," said Jeff, wondering if he could still wear his sunglasses for the meeting, but deciding that wouldn't work, even in PR.

"Morning, son," bellowed Wayne, slapping Jeff on the arm when he walked in. He flopped in the chair opposite Jeff, grinning in a manner that no man should be grinning in on Monday morning.

"What can I do for you, Mr. Summerville?"

"Call me, Wayne, Jeff. Have a cigar?" he asked, holding one of the vile concoctions out to Jeff, waving it under his nose. Jeff grabbed his stomach, making sure it was still there.

"No, thank you, sir. Wayne," he corrected.

"Good, good. We've got lots of things to worry about. I tell you, you are a miracle-working man. You should have seen Sheldon last night. Oh, my. Pretty as a picture, and just as grown-up as I think I've ever seen her."

"She *is* twenty-seven, sir. Wayne."

"I know, but sometimes…well, that's not what's important. But what is important is that you have *delivered*. We're all set for the papers to be signed on Friday and Sheldon will become officially betrothed. All that said, I'm a man who remembers the people who work for me, and the work they do." He pulled out his checkbook and started to write. "I think I owe you this. Wrecked the first one."

Jeff held up his hand. "No, thank you, sir. Wayne. It's all part of the job."

"Bull-honky."

"I mean it, sir."

Wayne tore the check out, and put it on the desk. "Consider it an advance payment for all that business I want to see floating your way. Summerville-Mason Consumer Products. I expect big things from Columbia-Starr Communications. Big things. Oh, I misspoke. Columbia-Starr-Brooks Communications. Can't forget that. That's key."

Jeff winced. "Of course, sir. Wayne."

Mr. Summerville rose and then slapped him on the

back. "I like you, son. You're good people. Did you know that?"

Jeff nodded.

After Wayne Summerville left, Jeff took the check and ripped it up into tiny pieces, then he popped four aspirin. But his head didn't hurt nearly as badly as his heart.

RIGHT AFTER HER MONDAY MORNING shopping trip to Bendel's, Jeff called her cell. He had two tickets to the Mets game and he thought it'd be good to correct the last impression that she'd made there. She almost said no, almost told him her impression was in fine shape, thank you very much, but she couldn't.

However, she did insist that she meet him at the stadium, rather than him picking her up from her apartment. She might be a masochist, but she wasn't into that much pain.

The stadium was packed, full of black, blue and orange, and this time, Sheldon had brought her Mets hat.

He was waiting for her in front of the will-call window, hands stuffed in jeans pockets, sunglasses hiding anything in his eyes, and a Mets cap on his head.

Just another Monday.

"Hey," she told him.

"Hey," he answered, and that was the extent of all scintillating conversation. She had a beer, he stuck to Coke, and even after the sun went down, he still wore his sunglasses.

"You okay?" she asked, finally.

"Sure," he answered. "Need a hot dog?"

"Yes, please."

Things were quiet until the fourth inning when the

bases were loaded, and Reyes was up at bat. Jeff pulled off his sunglasses and leaned forward in his seat.

Sheldon watched him, noticed the dark circles, the five o'clock shadow at his jaw, and wondered.

The pitcher sent two breaking balls, but at the third pitch, he took a chunk of it, sending it flying over the center field fence.

Jeff turned to her, smiled, and she thought how easy it would be to kiss him then. Just like before, caught up in the moment. He held still for a second, and then he must've realized she wasn't going to kiss him. His smile faded just a bit.

"Sorry," he murmured, shaking his head.

It should have felt like a great victory to Sheldon, but it didn't.

When the game was over, there was an awkward moment as they both waited on line for cabs to take them back into Manhattan.

"We could share a cab," offered Sheldon.

"That'd be good," answered Jeff.

The cabbie asked where they were headed. She said, "Battery Park" at the same time that he said "Upper West Side." Sheldon took a deep breath. "Upper West Side," she said. "That'll be fine."

He walked her to the awning, being very careful not to touch her. "I can go," he said. "I didn't mean to make assumptions. It's that—I wanted to see you again." He didn't look at her as he talked, his face in the shadow from the cap, but she could hear things in his voice that she wasn't supposed to hear.

"We'll have coffee," she told him.

"Coffee would be good."

When they got upstairs, he still didn't touch her. They were dancing around no-man's land, neither one wanting to assume too much or cause trouble.

She ended up making coffee, and he sat in her favorite chair, telling her about Andrew's engagement party. It was hard to listen when he looked so tired, and she wanted to comfort him, but she was afraid to comfort him. Everything seemed so close to the surface, so close to spilling over the edge. Finally she stood up, because she couldn't sit there and pretend.

"I'm going to take a shower. You can wait if you want."

He looked confused, but nodded.

Sheldon went to the bedroom, stripped off her clothes, and stepped under the steaming water. She didn't need a shower, she needed to cry, and here was the only place she could be alone. She stood under the warm spray, letting the water wash over her, but it didn't take away the pain.

She leaned against the wall, trying to pull herself together, when she heard the shower door open. Strong arms came around her, and he held her.

"I didn't want to assume," he whispered. "But I didn't want you to hurt."

For a long time they stood together, and she cried until she didn't have any more tears. When the tears were gone, he kissed her cheek, her neck, her mouth.

He took her in the shower, rough and hard, with only raw emotion, but she welcomed it. This, without the trappings of excess complications. When he was inside her, she didn't have to think, she only had to feel. He stayed with her all night, but when she woke up in the morning, he was gone.

THE SAM PORTER SHOW WAS FILMED at a television studio in New Jersey. Mercedes had never done a public affairs show before, hell, she'd never been on television before for that matter, but her agent was very excited and said it was "a good thing." The studio was smaller than she'd expected and they led her to a counter, where people did her makeup and hair as if she hadn't already spent three hours getting everything perfect, but no, she wasn't wearing the right shade of blush. So, she let them do their thing, and in the end, grudgingly, she admitted that maybe, possibly, they were right.

Okay, she looked awesome. There was liner around her dark eyes. She looked mysterious and sultry, and they'd used some amazing lipgloss, a great maroon shade. She pouted provocatively, and fantasized she was a secret agent who was using her body to coax the secrets of the world from some master spy.

Yeah, she was fine with a capital *F.*

At least Jeff would be there, glowering in the wings. He'd spent the afternoon coaching her, but she was still nervous.

He walked into the green room and stopped abruptly.

"You like?" she asked.

He snarled twice, which she took as code for yes.

"Do you remember what you're supposed to do?" he asked.

"Stay on point. We're discussing a cult of censorship that is rising all over the country, limiting freedom of speech and muzzling the voices of women everywhere. Women who want to explore their sexuality—"

"Can it, Mercedes."

"I was just practicing."

"And if he starts in on anything about Sheldon, what are you going to say?"

"No comment," answered Mercedes primly.

"All right. I can't believe you're doing this. You shouldn't be doing this."

"My agent said it'll be great. We have the book proposal going out next week, and she thinks this will tip it over to auction."

"Whatever."

"Do you not care about my illustrious literary career— a career that is only getting bigger by the second?"

He rubbed his eyes. "I'm sorry, Mercy. I haven't been sleeping."

"Nor eating either, I would presume. You're looking skinny."

"I'm eating fine, *Mom*."

"You don't want to go all manorexic."

"I'm fine, Mercedes."

He didn't look fine, something was eating at his insides like a cancer, a cancer that Mercedes suspected had long, blond hair and big, vapid blue eyes. Jeff normally had a sunny disposition, but now, well, now he was acting like Andrew. Completely un-fun. She missed the old guy.

Just then, a young girl, more of a teenager, came to the door.

"Mr. Porter will speak to you in five. He has some questions that he'd like to ask."

Then the girl disappeared.

"Did you hear that? Mr. Porter will speak to you in five. Like he's the Pope or something. What am I supposed to do, kiss his ring?"

"Don't get all pissy, Mercedes. Remember, you

have to stay calm. He's going to try and get you to lose your cool."

"Yeah. Sure. Whatever."

He gave her a look.

Five minutes later, the great Sam Porter came into the room and sat down across from her. It took her a second because she wasn't expecting someone so—so—male.

At that moment, she saw what millions of other American women already knew. Sam Porter was hot. He had this sandy brownish hair that appeared dark until the light hit it exactly right. And it was wavy, not straight, like the traditional Brooks hair. And his eyes were green, forest-green, a wise color. And then there was his mouth. No arguing there, the mouth was sexy. Kissable. Mercedes drew her gaze away.

"Ms. Brooks, glad to have you on the show," he said, shaking her hand, breaking the spell.

"It was good of you to invite me," she stated nicely.

"You know what we're here to discuss."

"Sex," she answered.

He frowned, although it wasn't quite a frown, it was more a bristling of eyebrows to indicate displeasure. "I wanted to talk about the effect of the smut culture on American society today, and whether young people are getting unduly corrupted by bad influences."

Mercedes felt her back stiffen, her blood heat, and if there were other, more sexual side-effects at work, she wasn't going to name them. "I don't think—" she started, and Jeff interrupted.

"Absolutely, and Mercedes is here to explain her side of the issue, in a fair, unbiased manner."

Sam frowned, and this time there was no bristling of

the eyebrows, it was an out-and-out frown. "Who are you?"

Jeff held out a hand. "I'm Ms. Brooks's media representative. Columbia-Starr Communications. Call me Jeff. Jeff Smith."

It was the first time Mercedes had seen her brother like this, one on one, and she was impressed. Oh, she'd seen him work the union strike, the magazine parties, but she'd never seen him like this. Not a party-animal type, but astute, sharp. Responsible. It was a pleasant surprise.

Sam looked at Mercedes with new respect in his eyes. "I wasn't expecting anyone else."

"Where I go, my people go," she stated, liking the way *my people* flowed off her tongue.

"You'll be on the show, too, Jeff?"

"I wasn't planning on it," answered Jeff.

"But I insist," added Mercedes.

Jeff glared, Sam frowned, and Mercedes smiled happily.

"He'll have to go through makeup," said Sam.

Jeff looked like he was about to argue. Mercedes gave him her big, sad eyes, and he nodded. Not happily, but still, he was her brother.

"The first segment will be a teenager who saved his brother from a fire. That'll be ten minutes, and then we cut to a woman from Rhode Island who is protesting unfair hiring practices at a home improvement store, and then we have you and Mr. Smith on for the last five minutes. We may have five minutes to take calls in there, too, unless the Rhode Island story is more interesting than it sounds."

"Lovely," said Mercedes, tossing back her hair.

Sam stood, and then went to go. Before he walked

out the door, he turned around and glanced at her. Mercedes raised an eyebrow. He shook his head and left.

"I can't believe you were hitting on him," said Jeff as soon as they were alone.

"I was not hitting on him, oh, you who will sleep with anything with breasts."

"You were hitting on him, Mercedes. He knew it. This isn't five o'clock happy hour at Bar Nine."

"Can you please stop seeking out the pleasures of the flesh whatever the subject matter may be?"

He stood up, hands flexing. "Mercedes, one day, I swear you're going to get in serious trouble, and there will be no one to bail you out. Not Andrew, not Mom, not even me."

"What is wrong with you? You're a fun person, Jeff. But for the past two weeks, you've been really, really, really cranky. Almost as bad as Andrew, and you know that's bad."

His eyes lost some of their steam, and Mercedes noticed the circles under them. "What's wrong, Jeff? Is this because of Sheldon? Do I need to kick her ass?"

He shook it off. "No," he answered. "I've got stuff going on at work."

"Well, stop it, then. It's making you yuck."

He tried to smile. "Yeah, don't want to be yuck."

Mercedes gave him her best look of comfort, but she knew better. No, Jeff had severe heart problems, and she wasn't even sure he knew it. Given Jeff, he probably thought it was a stomach ulcer. Man, he was such a—

"We're ready, Ms. Brooks," said the girl from the doorway, and she led Jeff and Mercedes to the set.

"We'll wait right here until Sam's ready."

Mercedes noticed the way the girl slipped Sam's name past her lips. The girl was majorly crushing on her boss, and probably Mr. Porter was screwing her brains out when the cameras stopped rolling. Popping her up on the desk, and pounding inside her until she was screaming for—

"Ready?" asked the girl.

Mercedes cleared her head. "Yes."

The cameras cut to commercial, and Mercedes and Jeff went to their seats.

The stage manager started counting down, and Mercedes realized that she was terrified. God, this was live television.

Jeff grabbed her hand. "It's going to be fine," he whispered.

"Three-two-one," said the stage manager, and then he disappeared.

"And now on tonight's program, we're here talking with Mercedes Brooks, and her media representative, Jeff Smith. Mercedes is the author of the notorious *Red Choo Diaries,* a sex blog full of titillating gossip and stories about people, real and imagined, within the New York area." Then he turned to her, and flashed her a warm smile. "Miss Brooks, welcome to the show."

"Thank you, Sam," she said, and then nodded at the audience.

"Now first of all, it seems to me, and I'm just a man with humble opinions, but it seems to me, that all this, well, forgive me, but *smut,* isn't helping with America trying to compete with the rest of the world, unless we're talking about sex. However, with our schools lagging behind, our businesses lagging behind and our economy doing the same, do you really believe that people need another meaningless pastime to detract them from day-to-day work?"

"Sex is another meaningless pastime?" Mercedes laughed. "You don't have a girlfriend, Mr. Porter, do you?"

"We can keep my personal life out of this, Ms. Brooks. Actually, I don't think you're answering my question. What about education? What about scientific and technological achievement? Pardon me for saying, but I don't think we can cure cancer from the missionary position, if you get my drift."

"Oh, I get your drift, Mr. Porter," said Mercedes and under the desk, Jeff squeezed her thigh. Hard. Okay, back to the points he coached her on. "What I provide is entertainment, nothing more."

"But you know, and I'm speaking as a man here, when you start walking on the physical appetites road, the endorphins start firing in the brain. One scintillating thought. Zap. Maybe a story, or a movie. Boom. And pretty soon all you want are those pinging explosions going off in your brain. It's chemistry, Ms. Brooks. And I don't think Americans can afford to lose any more of their brains to fun and excitement."

"And your show, Mr. Porter? Is it fun and excitement, or is it curing cancer?"

Sam leaned in close and she got a tiny hint of his cologne. "I'm here to educate people, Miss Brooks."

"You're not here to entertain them, Mr. Porter?"

He held up his hands. "Okay, I can see we aren't going to reconcile that, so let's change topics. Your blog has a habit of telling stories, very personal stories about people in the New York area."

"I don't use real names."

"Well, no, but it's not hard to figure out. For instance, last week you wrote about a sultry, blond-haired heiress, and unless you've been living in outer Bolivia, and I don't want to offend any outer Bolivian viewers, but unless you've been living pretty far away, it's not hard to ascertain that we're talking about Sheldon Summerville, whose father happens to be one of the richest men in America."

"I don't think we need to discuss this," Jeff spoke up. "As a fellow media professional, surely you can see that naming names isn't going to help the situation you've been describing."

"But Ms. Brooks might as well have come out and said it. I mean, we all know who she's talking about. And when *The Red Choo Diaries* heats up with stories of a beach in the Hamptons, well, do you think Ms. Brooks is doing Ms. Summerville any favors? I mean, come on, she's describing—in elaborate detail I might add—exactly what sexual proclivities Miss Summerville and her companion—"

Boom.

Mercedes completely missed Jeff jumping up, but she didn't miss the fist flying over the desk. Sam fell out of his chair, Jeff stalked off the stage, and Mercedes was left smiling apologetically for the camera.

"And to commercial," yelled the stage manager.

Mercedes stared at Sam, who had yet to come up off the floor. He was sitting on his side, rubbing his jaw. "Are you okay?" asked Mercedes, helping him to his feet.

The girl ran toward them, and hitched her arm around Sam's waist, helping him from the stage.

Sam turned around and pointed to Mercedes. "I want to talk to you. Now."

Obediently Mercedes followed.

"HOW MUCH DID YOU PAY HIM to do that?" Sam asked, once they made it back to the green room. "Jeff Smith. Hmm, that's not even his real name, is it? He's a bouncer, isn't he? You just wanted to get yourself plastered all over the news, and what better way than punching Sam Porter on a live television show."

"Now, wait a minute, mister. You were the one who started hitting below the belt. We were supposed to talk about sex in American culture, not Sheldon Summerville's bare breasts."

"I didn't bring up her breasts."

"Well, you were about to, before Jeff hit you."

Sam continued to rub his jaw, the reddened skin turning black and blue. "He's got a mean right hook."

"Yes, he does," answered Mercedes, not bothering to add that Jeff had taken boxing lessons in the ninth grade because he had a thing for the coach's daughter. "He's in love with her."

"Sheldon Summerville? Does she know him?"

"Intimately."

Softly, Sam began to laugh, and Mercedes warmed to him then. He had a nice laugh.

"Does it hurt?" she asked, pointing to his jaw.

"It throbs some," he replied.

"Do you have some ice in that refrigerator, or is all that for show?"

He nodded, and Mercedes took some cubes and

wrapped them in a paper towel. "Here, use this," she instructed, handing it to him.

He pressed the towel against his jaw. "Thanks."

Fascinated, Mercedes hopped up on the table, and watched as he finished cleaning his face. "Do you really believe all the things you said out there? Or was that for the ratings?"

He looked at her with impassive green eyes. "It's about control, not actions."

"And you're Mr. Self-Control."

"Uh-huh. It's not very hard when you try."

Mercedes smiled at him. "So if a woman comes on to you, you say no, whether you want to or not?"

"If I'm not involved with her, yes," he responded, but the green eyes were no longer so impassive. Mr. Self-Control was currently very curious.

Mercedes held out her hand and stroked his jaw. "Even if you want to say yes."

"You can stop now, Mercedes. I'm not interested in being written up in *The Diaries.*"

"But you *are* interested," she said. A pointed stare at the fly of his trousers revealed it was quite obvious what Mr. Self-Control was thinking.

"Yes, but you're only acting like this to prove a point."

Mercedes shrugged. "Maybe," she answered, because actually her motives weren't nearly that academic.

He stood up next to her, and trapped her, hands on either side. This time she definitely smelt his cologne, and she liked it. "You won't do anything. You're being a tease, aren't you? Mercedes Brooks, author of *The Red Choo Diaries,* and yet you never write about you, Mercedes, do you?"

Mercedes looked at him from beneath her lashes. "Maybe I'm the voyeur."

"You're a coward," he told her in a blunt-matter-of-fact voice. She could feel his breath whisper against her mouth.

"Am not." She wanted to sound defiant, but merely sounded, uh-hum, turned on.

He extended his hand toward her, long fingers inviting, and her mind flew to a thousand possibilities. All of them involving capable hands. "If I touched you, would it make it on the Internet, Mercedes?"

"It'd ruin your reputation," she said honestly, wondering if his hands were as capable as they looked. Her eyes met his and she saw the intent there, but no, he wasn't about to touch her.

Darn.

He dropped his hand, and Mercedes shook her hair in that way she'd picked up from Sheldon. From the outside, Mercedes appeared calm, collected, infinitely sophisticated. On the inside, she was a mess, but hey, acting ran in the family.

"We're not done, Mercedes." He all but threatened her, and the green eyes went dark, shaded with black and gold. They were startling. They were eyes that could hypnotize her with a single look. He released her.

"I'll see you in your dreams, Sam," she said, struggling for, then finding her balance.

He didn't say another word.

15

SUZIE Q WAS THE BEST PLACE IN the world for a man to forget about any particular woman. It was a gentlemen's club, with bare skin, overpriced drinks and smiles all around. Here, Jeff was surrounded by women. Beautiful, naked women paid well to be whatever a man desired. This time it wasn't working.

Jeff looked at his brother and tried desperately to infuse some life into this party.

"It's technically the last night of your freedom. You need to live it up. Kick up your heels. Paint the town red. All that crap."

"I'm engaged, Jeff. It's too late for freedom."

Jeff's mouth twisted in a hard line. "Not until you're married. You're not absolutely, one-hundred-percent, guaranteed untouchable until you're married. Until there's a wedding ring on the finger, you're still fair game."

"I trust Jamie, and I don't want to fool around."

"You didn't want to get married, and see what happened to that."

"You're wasting your money here. You're always wasting your money here. Why can't we go to a normal bar?"

"I thought we needed to spend quality time together."

"Here?"

"Why not?"

"How much do you want?"

"Can you stop that? I'm making it, damnit. In New York. On my own."

"Don't you even need money for a charity?"

"If it will make you feel loved, give me a minute and I'll think of something." Jeff stared at the stage, watching the mechanical gyrations of the dancer, and wondered what was wrong with him. His body should be loving this, but he was limp, lifeless, whipped. He took another drink of gin, downing the contents of the glass.

The waitress appeared, flashing a perfect set beneath his nose, and Jeff didn't even feel a pulse. "We'll take another round," he said, giving her an extra ten for absolutely no reason at all.

"I thought you were here for a good time," said Andrew, assuming his thinking look.

Jeff assumed the pose of a man having a good time, because they were here for a good time. Good times were to be had. Here. Surrounded by glistening flesh and pulsating, throbbing bodies. Jeff just needed to get with the program.

"Oh, yeah. Look at that," he said, pointing to the nearest, nudest chest. "I haven't seen breasts that prime since…" *Since last night.*

"…since a long time," he finished.

Andrew wasn't buying it for a minute. "Punch out any talk show hosts recently?"

"Screw you," he said, dropping all pretense of having a good time.

"You're getting famous. Did the boys at Columbia-Starr I.D. you as Jeff Smith?"

"I told them that I have a lot of look-alikes. I don't think they wanted to consider the alternative. My secretary knows, though."

"Will she blab?"

"He."

"You have a male secretary?"

"Don't even start, Andrew. The world's a different place, now. Get over it."

"I was playing golf with Ed Weinberger the other day and he brought up the VP job again."

"No," answered Jeff.

"You're being stupid. At least talk to the guy."

"I know how this works, Andrew. You pull a few strings, whoosh, doors open, and bingo, I'm CEO."

Andrew ate the olive from his martini. "Actually, it's only a VP position."

"Doesn't matter. I do my own thing. Just me. Nobody else." He shook his head and took a long swallow of his fresh drink. "All my life…" He trailed off because feelings were bubbling too close to the surface. Jeff had never liked feelings, life was easier without them.

"What?"

Jeff stared impassively at the stage, the colored lights hurting his eyes. "It's not important."

"It's important. Tell me."

"It's not important."

"What were you going to say?"

So Andrew wasn't going to give up. What did it hurt to explain, maybe then he'd finally figure out why Jeff kept turning down Weinburger's offers.

"Fine. I don't like being second string, Andrew. Any other household in America, and I'd be numero uno in all markets, but it's hard being little brother to a wunderkind."

"I didn't know."

"I know you didn't know. You wouldn't be you if you knew. And it's not like I don't appreciate you trying to take care of me—even though I'm over thirty—but I want to—no, I have to—make it on my own."

"All right."

Jeff stared suspiciously because Andrew didn't give in easily. He might say one thing, but underneath, steely determination remained. "No more job offers?"

"Then no more charitable contributions?" quipped Andrew.

Damn. Still, it felt good to joke, to laugh, to smile. God, it'd been forever. "Oh, come on. That's for the betterment of mankind. Who knows, you might even end up curing cancer—indirectly."

Andrew lifted his glass. "That'd be nice."

They watched the dancers for a while; Jeff stifled a yawn. Andrew would notice that. Besides, the gin was starting to kick in, giving him a nice, numbing glow.

"Mercedes says that Sheldon's engaged now."

"Not yet." Jeff looked at Andrew, warning him off the subject. "Mercedes has a big mouth."

"You're lucky she didn't put an engagement notice on the blog site."

"Don't give her any more ideas," said Jeff, hoping that this would change their topic of conversation.

"So, are you still working with Sheldon?" asked Andrew, not changing the topic of their topic of conversation.

"Nah. That's over."

"How over?"

"Over, over," said Jeff, downing more gin because he wanted the numbness back.

"Can I give you some advice?"

"No. Shut up and drink."

"Are you going to be like this for the rest of your life? Go out and get laid."

Jeff lifted his glass and stared at his brother through the golden haze of Tanqueray. "I tried. Didn't happen."

Andrew frowned. "Then you need to get her unengaged. Fast."

"She's not engaged," insisted Jeff. It was very important that everyone understand that right at this moment, Sheldon was not engaged.

"When?"

"Friday."

Andrew checked his watch. "The clock is ticking."

It was so easy for everyone to make a joke. Jeff was tired of trying to pretend, trying to make jokes, when nothing seemed funny. "Don't you think I know it? Don't you think it's killing me?"

"Have you told her?"

Jeff buried his head on the bar, fighting the urge to pound it against the polished wood. Eventually, he looked at his brother, pointing an unsteady finger at Andrew. "You know, you and Mercedes think it's all such a breeze. It is for you, and it is for her, and if it's not, she fakes it. 'Just tell her you love her and poof, all the problems disappear.' It's not that simple."

"What's not?" asked Andrew, the man who had never

shied away from complex problems. He lived for complex problems. Not Jeff.

"I'm not that way, Andrew. Hell, you're richer than anyone I know, and you're not even that way."

"What way are we talking about?"

"They go to *galas*. Buildings are named Summerville. Her father has a closetful of tuxedoes, and they're not rentals. And don't get me started on Sheldon," said Jeff, getting started on Sheldon. "I couldn't even afford to keep her in underwear."

"Maybe she doesn't care about being kept in underwear," said Andrew in a calm voice. Jeff didn't understand how any man could talk about Sheldon and underwear in a calm voice.

"You don't know Sheldon. She loves her underwear." He gave up trying to explain. "I can't do it. I can't say, 'Honey, about that eight-hundred-dollar haircut.'" He reached out to down more alcohol, but Andrew stopped him.

"At least give her a choice, Jeff."

"I'm not a choice. Not for her."

"You're worth more than that."

Yes, words of wisdom from the six-billion-dollar man. No one seemed to believe that Jeff wasn't designed to be anything more than a PR flack. Jeff knew deep in his soul that he was supposed to cruise through life with the top down, a marketing smile plastered on his face, maybe cracking some punchlines along the way. He was the freeloader, running a million places behind Andrew, and it didn't matter how hard he worked, or how fast he ran, he wasn't going to be any more than that.

Ever.

Sheldon didn't need another weight hanging around her neck, and that was all Jeff would be. He could imagine the looks they would get. This is what she settled for? Harvard? No. Lawyer? No. Public relations, they would whisper in a shocked tone of voice. She could do better than that.

Josh for instance.

Jeff swore and kept swearing, giving in to everything vile that was raging inside him. Finally, he was all sworn out. "I just came here to get drunk and eyeball naked women."

"Does it help?"

Jeff ordered another round of drinks, and this time Andrew didn't cut him off. "No, but I'm going to keep trying. Someday. Maybe."

"SHEL-L-L-L-LDON!!!"

She heard the voice shouting outside her apartment door, and then the buzzer sounded. Loud, long. Someone was sitting on her buzzer. Two guesses, and one of them wasn't Josh.

Sheldon got up out of bed and stalked to the door, flinging it open.

Jeff.

One very woozy Jeff. His shirt was undone, his hair was ruffled, like someone's fingers had stroked it. Not hers. She took a step back because she didn't want to think about that. Didn't want to think about Jeff having a life outside her.

He threw back his head and howled. "Shel-l-ldon!" This time she pulled him into the apartment.

He grinned at her, an expression completely devoid

of humor, and Sheldon watched him warily. This wasn't the Jeff she knew—the clothes were messed, the veneer was gone, the polished sheen was missing. All that was left was him. She had always wanted to know what lurked beneath the surface. Now she did.

"What the hell are you doing?" she asked, sounding a lot braver than she felt.

He walked toward her, backing her against the wall. "Whatever I want," he answered, and with one hand ripped the front of her tank-top. His face looked harsh, like he didn't care. But his eyes betrayed him, telling her he was a liar.

"Feel better?" she asked, like she didn't care, either.

"No. I hurt, Sheldon," he said, his body tight against hers. She felt him, felt his heart pounding, felt the hard ridge against her thigh, felt the hurt, too. An open wound, exposed so much like hers. She wanted to stroke his face, wanted to kiss his lips, wanted to soothe him. Her hands stayed at her side.

His hand grasped one breast roughly, and she clamped her jaw tightly until the pain passed.

"That makes two of us," she managed, using her calmest, gentlest voice.

He put his mouth to the top of her breast and sucked. Hard. She bit her lip, but wasn't about to give him the satisfaction of a reaction. "There," he said, studying the purple bruise on her skin. "Explain that to your fiancé."

"He's not my fiancé."

"Yet." He looked at her, his eyes red and wet. "Has he touched you, Sheldon?"

Sheldon thought about the one kiss she and Josh had shared, saw the demon in Jeff's eyes. "No."

"Idiot," he said, and then proceeded to mark her other breast, too. Sheldon stood and endured. It was what she did best.

"Do you know what I would do if you were mine?" he said, resting his head against her breast.

"What?" she asked, raising a hand to stroke the dark strands.

"This," he said, and then wrapped her legs around his jeans-clad waist.

If she were stronger, maybe she would say something. Tell him she loved him. Maybe she wouldn't. She elected to stay silent. Another Sheldon specialty.

"Do you know what I did tonight?" he said, pressing closer toward again. She smelled the perfume, the alcohol on him, and she didn't really want to know. Didn't want to hear, but maybe if she did, maybe if it was something awful, her life could move forward without him. Anything was worth a shot. "What?"

"I was surrounded by beautiful women. Naked, beautiful women. Gorgeous. I wanted so bad to find someone. Lose myself inside them, even for a few minutes, just to escape. I wanted peace. And do you know what happened?"

"I don't want to know," she answered, because in the end, it didn't matter. She wouldn't move forward without him. Ever. Even now, with this, it didn't change anything. It was a moment of clarity for her, because she knew if he came to her after she was married, she wouldn't say no then, either.

Wedding ring or not.

"You want to know, Sheldon. You need to know this. Nothing happened. I couldn't. I'm going to be the only thirty-two-year-old treated for erectile dysfunction." He pushed hard against her. She gasped.

"This doesn't feel like erectile dysfunction," she managed between clenched teeth.

He smirked. "That's because it's you."

"Why am I so different?" she asked. It was a bad idea to taunt him right then, but she couldn't help it, she needed to twist the night. He wanted to hurt her, she would hurt him right back.

"What am I going to do?" he asked.

"What are we going to do?" she corrected.

His body relaxed, his hands gentled, and he braced his forehead against hers. "What are *we* going to do?"

He released her legs, and she stood, barely. Then she kissed him, because she loved him. Because he loved her. He looked at her once, then pulled her shirt together. "I should go."

She nodded, because she needed to think. He opened the door and left, and Sheldon pulled off her ripped top, holding it to her face. Alcohol, someone else's perfume and him.

It hurt, but the hurt was better than nothing.

JEFF WOKE UP FROM A VERY pleasant dream. Sheldon was talking to him, her voice seductive yet still firm and unbending. He felt a whap on his head and opened his eyes.

Okay, it was Sheldon. He rolled his shoulders, wondering why he was so stiff. When he looked around, he got his answer. He was sitting in her hallway.

"Security called me at five and asked about the strange man sleeping outside my door."

"You should have woken me up."

"It was more fun watching you sleep."

He noticed the high-cut blouse she wore and the tension in her face. And something new. Joy. "I'm sorry," he said, rubbing his eyes, wishing he could rub out his troubles. He had so much to make up to her, so much that he could never make up to her. He'd always only be good, never good enough.

The day before her engagement and now his mind was full of wishes, full of things he wanted to give her, but nothing he had would make it.

"You remember?"

He rose, met her eyes. "Enough to know I won't forget it. You don't deserve that. You don't deserve my crap."

"No, I don't," she admitted. "Come inside. Get some coffee."

"Aspirin?" he asked hopefully, sensing a truce in the air, not sure why he deserved it.

She made a fresh pot of coffee. "You do that well." He was surprised that she looked at home in her kitchen. "Don't you have servants?"

"Nah. For one person? I think that's extreme."

Jeff shrugged. "Just asking. Plans for the day?" He admitted it was a desperate, needy question, and he didn't want to sound desperate and needy.

"Nothing."

"We should do something. Outside."

"Sure," she said casually, pouring his coffee with a trembling hand.

"I'm sorry."

"Once is enough, Jeff."

"Won't go there again."

She laid a hand over his. "Friends?"

He covered hers with his. "Forever."

TODAY WAS SHELDON'S LAST DAY of freedom, and she wanted to savor it like a last meal. By mid-morning tomorrow, she would be engaged. But for today, she could pretend everything was perfect.

She tucked her hair under a Yankees cap, and he wore a Mets hat. He wore Nikes, she wore heels. Until they got to Central Park, and then, well, the heels had to go, and he bought her a pair of ballet shoes at a souvenir shop just outside Central Park. She pirouetted for him. He laughed.

"You wanted to be a ballet dancer, too?"

She gave him her best Shakira moves. "Pop star."

He rubbed his eyes with his palms. "Don't give up the day job."

She should have been offended, but whenever he looked at her, offended was the last thing she felt. Cherished, that was what she felt. She pulled him up from the park bench. "Dance with me," she said, because they had never danced together, and it was suddenly important to check off all the things they hadn't done before.

He pulled her in a mock waltz. "There's no music."

"Yes, there is," she said, sure that she could hear the music in the air.

"I don't hear a thing. Except for the cop cars, the bull-dozers, and the eighty million school kids that are looking at you strangely."

She twirled in his arms. "I don't care."

He smiled and humored her. "It's your day."

The schoolkids moved past, identical yellow camp

shirts, backpacks and waterbottles. She and Jeff weren't alone, but it felt alone.

The music in her head slowed, soothed. She moved closer, and he didn't flinch. Not this time. Instead, he brought his arms around her, and they swayed back and forth, keeping time to a rhythm that no one else heard.

She felt his lips soft on her hair, and she closed her eyes, seeing a different world, a different place where there was no pain, no hurt. Things simply were. *They* simply were.

His heart beat solidly underneath her hand, and she left her fingers there, a peaceful smile on her face. The sun warmed her. The hazy days of summer. With every imaginary beat in her head, she fell deeper and deeper into him, not so imaginary.

He stopped moving, tilted her chin, kissed her. The music played in her head, louder, sweeter. She wound her arms around him even tighter, buried her fingers in the dark silkiness that lay against his neck. Maybe she couldn't tell him, maybe he couldn't tell her, but it was there, in her kiss.

In his kiss.

"We need to go," he whispered.

She didn't want to go. She wanted to stay, stop time for a moment. Be in a place where they could kiss in public, and no one would blink. Where he could touch her in public, like she was his. *Because she was his.*

She nodded once and wanted to take his hand. Walk together, like lovers. But they didn't. They walked next to each other like friends. Nothing more. He did a good job, but his eyes lingered longer than they should, and every now and then, her fingers accidentally grazed his.

It was going to be like this from now on, and she

fought to keep a smile on her face. They made the short walk to her apartment, and as soon as the door closed and the world was gone, she was in his arms again. His lips covered hers, and she stopped worrying about everything else.

Just now she needed to live for this. He took her on the floor, not waiting for the bed. She didn't care. The first time, they were still dressed.

The second time, the clothes were gone. Skin to skin, mouth to mouth. She took him inside her easily, closing her eyes, pretending they were a real couple. Pretending it wasn't Thursday, maybe Monday, maybe a day where time didn't exist. She smiled against his mouth, pressing fevered lips against his.

"Shush," he said, pressing his mouth to her tears.

"Stay here," she whispered when he pulled out of her. He thought she meant sex; she meant forever. His mouth loved her, no words, no promises.

She made promises. In her heart, they were there. When he pressed her back against the carpet, they were in her eyes.

He wanted to move to the bed, but she was terrified he would leave and so she kept him there, next to her, where she could touch him whenever she wanted, where she could kiss him whenever she wanted.

Didn't he know?

Maybe. For the rest of the afternoon, he loved her well. Over and over they went, until eventually the sun began to set.

"You'll stay?" she asked, her voice catching.

He rose, began to pull on his clothes, and she hated the sun for leaving her. Hated the sunset for coming too soon. This wasn't supposed to end. Forever, that's what he had said. But he hadn't promised.

He pulled her to her feet, held her, and then set her gently away. "Get dressed. Something nice."

"We're going out tonight?" she asked tightly. Sheldon didn't want to go out. This was it, their last night. She wanted to stay inside, sheltered, protected. Alone.

He nodded.

"I don't want to."

"Will you trust me?" he asked.

She shouldn't trust him. She knew she shouldn't trust him, but she did. She nodded.

"I'll be back in two hours."

"But—"

"Trust me," he pleaded, kissed her, then walked out the door.

JUST LIKE HE'D SAID, JEFF WAS back two hours later. In a tuxedo. She forgot to breath. She looked at his face, trying to read the secrets there. She only read the sadness there, and it terrified her.

He smiled at her, but it was his fake PR smile, only scaring her more. "Come here," he said, and led her downstairs.

"We don't need to go out," she argued, knowing this was a bad idea.

"You won't regret it," he answered.

He had a Town car waiting, and he helped her into the back seat. "Wait a minute, there's something you need." And he put a blindfold in front of her eyes.

Sheldon didn't like surprises, especially surprises like this. "Where are you taking me?"

"You'll see."

"Not at the moment."

"Give us a minute, Sheldon."

They rode in silence. He took her hand, his fingers wrapped around hers. She liked the warmth, the strength, the comfort. Eventually the car stopped, and she made a move to take off the blindfold.

He stilled her hands. "Not yet."

"I can't walk."

He lifted her in his arms. "Not a problem."

He carried her up stairs, and she heard padded carpet beneath his feet. However, she didn't hear voices, only silence. That was good. They were alone. Alone was important.

Then he put her down, and she felt wood underneath her feet. Wood that echoed when she walked. There were lights. Lights that burned hot on her skin. But everything was quiet. She reached out for him, and he took her hand.

"I needed to give you something," he told her. "But you have everything."

"Why did you need to give me something?" she asked, the detached sound of his voice making her panic.

"You know," he said.

"No, I don't," because she wanted him to say it.

"You know," he told her, and then he took a step away.

"You can look now." His voice was farther away.

She ripped off the blindfold, not sure what to expect. But not this.

The stage was wooden and round. Banks of lights formed a circle around her, an ivory arch was loomed high at her back. The Stern Auditorium. In front of her, the empty seats were maroon. She blinked. There were people there. Just a few. Some she recognized, some she didn't.

"What am I supposed to do?"

He stood below her in the pit. "You're supposed to play."

Her feet were frozen to the spot. She was terrified to hear the echo of her steps on the stage. Her music would be a slap in the face to the giants that had stood her before. "I can't play."

He gave her a hard look.

"But—"

"No. You have an audience. You don't want them to think you suck. If you want to do this more often, you're going to have to do better."

"I can't."

"You can," he argued. He pointed to her violin, the music, the stand. "It's all here. I'm going to go listen," he said, and the lights in the hall went dark. Except for the spotlight on her.

"Jeff?" she whispered. No answer.

She wanted to run away. Yet…

People would know the truth about her. Realize she couldn't play.

But she could play.

She could do this. All she had to do was pretend. Sheldon was a great pretender.

She went over and picked up her violin, the instrument solid in her hands. This was what she knew.

She bowed, like Stefan had taught her, and there was applause from the hall. It echoed loudly in her ears, and she searched for Jeff in the darkened auditorium, but it seemed as if it was her alone.

Not knowing what else to do, she began to play. First she played Beethoven, then Schubert, and then Brahms. And because she wasn't sure how long she was supposed to stay up on the stage, she played Bach, too.

And when she finished, the applause started.

She looked out in the audience, but the world was blurry, and she wiped her eyes, wanting to see, she really needed to see.

"Jeff?" she asked, but he wasn't there.

Mercedes walked up the aisle, along with an older woman with dark eyes and a familiar smile. She knew those eyes. The eyes that said that the Mets could come from behind and Sheldon could play at Carnegie Hall.

"Very nice, dear. I specially loved the Brahms."

"Thank you," she acknowledged, trying to be polite, but her nerves were shot to hell. She looked at Mercedes. Where's Jeff?"

"He's already left. This was supposed to be your time."

"He didn't say goodbye?" she said, clutching her violin to her because that was all she had left.

This was goodbye.

Oh, God. Her legs worked to stand. She had thought they could be together. Okay, she'd be engaged, then married, but did that matter? She didn't have scruples and honor.

Jeff did.

And the truth hit her. He had done more for her than anyone else, he had known her more intimately than any person ever had before. Tonight, he'd made his choice, and she wasn't part of it.

"There's a car for you outside," said Mercedes.

Sheldon dashed to the waiting vehicle, hoping he

was there. The driver took her home, and she searched her apartment, hoping he was there.

Nothing. Her last night of freedom was over, and she was alone.

She leaned against the wall, her knees buckling, and she slid down, buried her head against her knees, and quietly fell apart.

HIS MOTHER FOUND HIM IN the balcony, sitting quietly by himself. "Why are you making an old woman walk up all these steps? Up here with the bats and Quasimodo. I always loved that movie."

She settled in the seat next to her son and patted his hand.

"You're not old, Mom."

"You were always the best liar in the family, Jeff." She stared at the darkened stage, then gave him a knowing look. "How long were you planning to sit here?"

"Not much longer," he lied.

"All night, hmm?"

His lips curved into a smile. "What are you doing here? You should be at home in bed."

"And miss the show? I always loved this old hall. The magic, the talent. It was a place where people came to live out their dreams."

"It's nice."

"She's nice. The tabloids are hard on her."

"Yeah."

"Did you tell her yet?"

"What?" he asked, staring ahead, not daring to look at his mother.

"That you love her."

There it was. That word again. He hated that word, because he had never imagined that he could ever fall in love. He'd always believed that the emotional short-hand in his life would rob him of anything true and meaningful. His friendships were superficial, his relationships even shallower.

Ha. Surprise.

He'd fallen in love and love sucked. It hurt, it mocked you, made you realize all your shortcomings, all your flaws. He didn't know why people got so fired up about something that carved up your insides. "I haven't said anything to her."

"That's a pity."

Yeah, it was a pity. "She's better off this way."

"I don't believe that."

He didn't want to argue with his mom, they had always had a good relationship, but she had never interfered before. "Do you know the life she'll have? The things he can give her?"

"Bet he doesn't rent out Carnegie Hall."

"He could."

"It doesn't mean anything if it's not done with love."

"He'll love her. He won't be able to stop it."

"He's not you."

"You're my mother. Your opinion doesn't count."

"I'm going to tell you a secret, and you can't tell Andrew or Mercedes because it would cause all kinds of problems. You were always my favorite, Jeff, and you know why?"

"Why?"

She cleared her throat, just like when she was re-hearsing for a part. Then she started to speak, her mother voice. Her voice. "I was a single mom for a long time. Mercedes was born right after your father went out the door, and I didn't want to be a secretary, or a school-teacher, or a nurse. I wanted to be an actress. And when you have three little mouths to feed, and two of those are boys, a woman feels a lot of guilt, because acting jobs aren't the best for bringing in the groceries."

Jeff covered her hand, noticing the wrinkles and the thinning skin. His mother was getting old and he hadn't even noticed. He brought her hand to his lips. "You were a good actress. If we'd been in California, you would have made it."

"This is my monologue, don't interrupt."

"Go on."

"Thank you. Now, as I was saying, Andrew was great. Whatever we needed, he'd find a way. But he never believed in my acting. Never. He always thought I was a flighty old bird without a single thread of common sense."

"You're not old."

Thea shook her head. "Thank you for that moment of flattery. When I'd come back from an audition, and I didn't get the part, you'd take my hand, and look at me with that smile full of magic and tell me that every-thing was going to be all right because you believed in me. And I always knew that I would because you had faith in me. I needed that faith."

"I didn't do that, Mom. You're making up the whole thing."

"Yes, you did. The time I tried out for *Annie Get Your Gun,* you told me that I should have gotten the part because I sang better than Ethel Merman ever could."

"Ethel Merman?"

"This is my story, don't ruin it."

"Those were just words from a kid."

"But I needed those words, Jeff. Those words made the difference between a good life and a great life. I had a great life."

"You're still the best, Mom."

Not content with his flattery, she went in for the kill. "So when are you going to tell her you love her?"

"Leave it alone."

"She seems like a smart girl."

"She is."

"When are you going to show some faith in yourself?"

Jeff was tired of having this same discussion with everyone. With Andrew, with Mercedes, but never with Sheldon. She understood him better than anyone. She wasn't going to ask him to step up to the plate, and he wasn't going to ask her to step down from the guillotine. Stalemate.

"I can't ask her to give up all this. That's not faith, Mom, that's idiocy."

"If she loves you, it won't matter."

"Spoken like a woman who was perpetually poor."

"You're as stubborn as your brother."

"I thought I was your favorite."

"Where'd you get the money to rent this joint? Andrew?"

"I know a guy," said Jeff smoothly.

"You may be a good liar, but don't think your mother doesn't know when you're trying to pull one over on her."

"Don't worry. I won't starve. I had some cash stashed away."

"Your boat fund?"

"It wasn't actually a boat fund. More like extra cash that I didn't know what to do with. I knew I'd find a good cause, and I did."

"You are so far gone you actually believe your own shit."

"You're not supposed to swear."

"You're not supposed to be so foolish."

"Good night, Mom."

"Good night, son. Don't stay up too late."

JEFF DIDN'T SLEEP THAT NIGHT. He sat in Carnegie Hall until they kicked him out early Friday morning. Usually he was the first one to leave parties, never wanting to overstay his welcome, but now he didn't want to leave. The security guard shone a flashlight in his eyes, waking him up from a sweet dream.

"They're cleaning up, sir."

Jeff rose, cleared the fog from his brain. "Thank you," he said.

"Did you have a nice evening?"

"Very nice."

The guard rocked back on his heels. "Didn't know there was a concert here last night. Thought the schedule was clear."

"You should have heard her. I think she's the best in the world."

The man knew better than to believe him. "That's nice. You need to go home, sir."

Jeff checked his watch—9:00 a.m. He didn't have anywhere to go. She was signing over her life, and his life was pretty well over.

"Do you know your way, sir?" asked the guard,

because Jeff was simply standing at the aisle, staring at an empty stage.

She had played. She had gotten up there and done it. He had put even money on her not having the guts to do it, but he was wrong. He was so wrong. Sheldon, who thought she could do something, who thought she was schlub extraordinaire had done something extraordinary, something great.

He always knew that she could, had always believed in her. Just like she had always believed in him.

He began to smile. Then he began to grin.

"Yeah. Yeah, I think I do."

AT EXACTLY SEVEN MINUTES AFTER eleven, Sheldon was seated at a conference room table with four lawyers, her father, James Conrad and Josh. It wasn't the most romantic moment in her life, but hell, she was strong, she'd kicked butt at Carnegie Hall. Now she knew that she could do anything.

Josh had brought a ring. A big, emerald-cut yellow diamond on a platinum band. She hated it. She smiled at him and slipped it on her finger. "It looks wonderful."

"I wasn't sure," he started.

She cut him off. "You did fine."

Her father looked at her, maybe seeing something new in her face. "You're sure?"

And this was it, her last chance to back out. Her last chance to go back to Sheldon the schlub. No more. "Positive."

He studied her, blue eyes worried, but then he nodded. "All right."

The lawyer handed her the papers, a long sheaf of

legal words that blurred in front of her. He tried to explain, she interrupted him. At this rate, they would be here all day, discussing a cold-blooded exchange of cash and stock. Sheldon wasn't there, yet.

She smiled politely. "Just tell me where to sign," she said, and picked up the pen.

Then she put it down, because even though her back was to the door, she knew the moment Jeff walked into the room.

Was it always going to be like this?

He was still in the tux, the tie hanging dashingly to one side, but the sadness was gone from his face.

He looked right at her. "You haven't signed?"

She shook her head but not daring to hope. There was optimistic, and then there was stupid.

He came and stood next to Wayne Summerville, a head taller, a fortune lighter, and she loved him just as much.

"I've come to see if your daughter would marry me."

"You?" asked her father, not as shocked as Sheldon would have thought.

"You?" echoed Josh's father, not nearly as nicely, and Wayne shushed him with a hand.

Sheldon began to smile, a small smile that she was careful not to let Josh notice, but it was there all the same.

Jeff stuck his hands in his pockets. "Yes, sir."

"Do you consider yourself suitable for my daughter?"

"No, sir."

":Why not?"

"Well, I quit my job this morning."

"Really?"

"If I showed up here, they would fire me for blowing the account, and I felt like it would look better on my resumé if I resigned. I am pretty good at public relations. Something of a miracle worker," he answered. His smile wasn't the usual smooth, PR smile. This was nervous. Jeff was nervous. Sheldon smiled more.

"Yeah, but do you have another job waiting for you?"

"No, sir. Andrew lined up something for me, but I think I'd like to find something on my own. Without his help."

"Very smart."

"Not really."

"Who's Andrew?"

"Andrew Brooks, my brother."

"Andrew Brooks is your brother?" repeated Sheldon's father, surprised, and Sheldon wondered who Andrew Brooks was.

"Don't get excited, sir. I don't have his financial savvy."

But her father was still smiling. "I'm assuming you have some money in the bank to cover this downturn in your finances."

"No, sir. Blew it all recently. It was my boat fund, but uh, something else came up."

Right then, Sheldon put her hand under the table and slipped off the four-carat-ugly-as-a-mother diamond ring. Josh would have to find another Mrs. Conrad. She suspected one already existed, but he wasn't ready to admit it.

"Not very bright, boy, are you?"

"No, sir. Of my family, I'm probably the dimmest one, although I'd appreciate it if you didn't tell my sister that, because I usually pretend otherwise."

"You're not selling yourself very well."

"I do very good with things that don't mean anything. With the more important things, not so much."

"I see. Do you love my daughter?"

"Yes, sir. I was slow to come to that conclusion, or I would have been here earlier."

"And you want her to marry you?"

"Yes, above anything else in the world, but I think it's more important that she has a choice. That's why I'm here. No one gave her a choice, and I want her to have a choice."

"You don't think what I did was very nice?"

"I think you had her best interests at heart," replied Jeff, not quite answering the question.

"And you're not her best interests?"

"Absolutely not, sir."

"But you want to marry her."

"Yes, sir."

"Even if you're not her best interests?"

"Yes, sir. I believe I told you I was the dim one."

"Mr. Brooks, you've impressed me."

"So I can marry her?"

"Oh, no," her father said, shaking his head, his blue eyes sparkling. "I'm going to let her decide," he added, and Sheldon let go of the breath she was holding. "You were right," he told Jeff.

"I was?"

"Yes, sir. She needs a choice." Then her father clapped his hands, a man used to having his ordered obeyed, but in the nicest possible way. "I think we should clear out the room for a minute. James, you and I will have some new things to talk over."

The room emptied, except for Sheldon. Except for Jeff.

"You love me?" she asked, because she wanted him to say it.

Jeff nodded.

"That's not good enough. You have to tell me. In words, complete sentences. I've been waiting my entire life for you to tell me."

He smiled, a halfway smile that she hadn't seen in too long, and her heart let loose with a gentle sigh. "I love you, Sheldon."

"Why now?" she asked. "What changed your mind?"

"If you can play at Carnegie Hall and completely not suck, then maybe I can deal. I can't give you lots of underwear or eight-hundred-dollar haircuts. Can you survive that?"

"Do you think I love you?" she asked, dodging his question with one of her own.

"I'd like to think so."

"Why?"

"We're good together, Sheldon. I don't want another woman, and I'm too young to give up on sex."

She glared.

But he continued. "And I want to grow old with you. I want you to have violin lessons."

"Violin lessons?"

"I won't be able to take you on a round-the-world cruise, and the penthouse will probably have to go, but I think someday we'll have a boat."

She stayed silent, thinking, considering, in general, putting him through all the hell he put her through. In the end she didn't have a choice.

"I love you, Jeff Brooks."

"You're not very smart, Sheldon. That man sitting in there can give you anything."

"I already have everything. Except for the one thing I need to breath. I need you. I need you to prod me, shove me, bring me down from the glass shelf. I need you to love me."

He wrapped strong arms around her, kissing her like he wasn't going to let her go. Finally, forever.

"You had me going for a minute," he said, after he lifted his head.

"Good."

"But you're okay with this? It's not going to easy, Sheldon."

She gave him a long, thoughtful look. "I'm tired of easy, Jeff. I want to try something new. I can do more than I thought. I'm not really a schlub, you know."

He looked at her, respect in his eyes. Jeff looked at her that way now, and soon everybody was going to look at her the same way. She laughed and kissed him again. Because she could.

There was a discreet knock at the door, and then her father entered.

"Sheldon? What do you want to do?"

"I think I want to marry Jeff, Daddy."

He shook his head. "Damnit all, I knew something was up. I suppose I need to get you employed, boy."

Jeff looked at her father squarely, a determined glint in his eye. "No, thank you, sir. We'll be fine."

AND THEY *WERE* FINE. JEFF found a job with another firm, Cami broke up with Lance after she fell in love— again. This time with a responsible doctor. The Summervilles were over the moon.

Sheldon wasn't employed yet, but she had some ideas. She was nervous about them, because they would involve intelligence, determination, and courage, but every time Jeff looked at her, she knew she could.

Sheldon introduced herself to the other students in her chamber group, this time as Sheldon rather than as Sarah, and she also learned to live without underwear.

In fact, one evening, when they were settled on the carpet in Jeff's Battery Park apartment, he was exploring that very aspect of her personality.

He traced the lines of her skin, admiring the curves that looked more beautiful than she would ever know. He didn't like that he couldn't give her the things she deserved; still, she was happy. "So, when do you want to get married?" he asked casually.

She rose up on her elbows and stared. "We don't have to, if you don't want it. It's enough that you love me. Marriage is only a piece of paper," she said, and then shrugged her shoulders, as if she didn't care.

"No way. It's the full deal. Everyone has been raving about this marriage thing. I gotta do it."

"Yeah?" she asked him carefully.

Jeff gathered his courage, and then padded over to the dresser. Then he pulled out a velvet box, bent down on one knee and bowed his head in front of her. She still felt like a queen to him, and he wasn't sure why she wanted him, but she did. "Marry me."

Her hand stroked his cheek, lifted his chin, and when he looked up, her eyes were swimming with tears, no longer vapid and vacant, and his heart stopped—just for a moment, just as it always did. He saw his future in those eyes.

"Forever?" she asked, as if could ever leave her.

For once in his life, there were no words. No promises

good enough for her, no way to spin a phrase. He looked at her and simply nodded, love shining in his eyes. It was all he had, all he could give her.

Sweetly she came into his arms, as if she belonged there, because she did. Sheldon was his. Tonight. Tomorrow.

Once and for all.

Forever.

* * * * *

Don't miss the final entry of
The Red Choo Diaries, BEYOND SEDUCTION
featuring Mercedes Brooks
Available from Harlequin Blaze May 2007!
Turn the page for a sneak peek!

1

"OKAY, SAM, THAT'S A WRAP."

Sam Porter slid his chair back from the stage desk, took a last drink of water, and wanted nothing more than to be home, in bed, preferably alone, nursing a cold beer, and watching the tape of today's show.

Four am was too early for any human being of sound mind to be up, but he'd sacrificed in order to prep for tonight's interview. The interview had been a slam-dunk, the Jersey Senator was toast, but now Sam felt like death warmed over, although the night was still young. He nodded in the general direction of the producer. "Thanks, Kristin. See you tomorrow."

The crew started to leave. Goodbyes were always the shortest when the weekend was lurking.

Kristin winked at him and put aside her clipboard and headset. "Maybe you'll see me. Got a hot date. I think I'm going to elope."

He rubbed at his face with his palms. "Just as long as you're back Monday morning. Don't make me break in another producer."

"Sure, boss," she answered.

After Kristin took off, looking gloriously happy, because obviously she didn't get up at four a.m., Sam

headed for the dressing room. Finally, a chance to lose
the suit. He pulled on his jeans with a blissful sigh. He
would never be a suit, and, although he played a
talking-head on TV, and did it well, denim was his
natural habitat.

The studio was a cold, mechanized place with three
cameras, overhead banks of monitors, and the smell of
sanitized air freshener, rather than the smell of hard
work. Sam's dad had been a plumber, who came home
smelling of grease and somebody's drain pipe. Sam had
learned to appreciate the smells that came with an
honest day's labor. And they weren't air freshener.

He kept his dressing room computer and air freshener
free. His ratty, overstuffed couch was always waiting for
him when he needed to lay down and think, and the
sounds of Bob Dylan, the Killers, and Springsteen were
always on his iPod to drown out the noise. At his heart,
Sam was a Jersey boy, born and bred, and although Manhattan paid his salary, his home sat on the other side of
the Hudson. When he came in the room, he cast a longing
look at the couch, but had places to go and people to
meet. The couch — and sleep would have to wait.

Two long East-West blocks covered the distance
from the studio to the bar on 11th where he was headed.
A few fans stopped, waved, but New York wasn't really
the target market for the Sam Porter show. A conservative talk show host in Manhattan garnered more death
threats than autograph requests. Since Sam was a firm
believer in the right to bear arms, as well as carry them,
he wasn't phased.

The cool, November air blew around and through the
cement jungle. It was a great night for a walk, the perfect

way to wake him up. Midtown was bustling. Cabs were lined up bumper to bumper, the night lights began to illuminate the sky. Yeah, city life was okay.

He passed by a bookstore, and a photograph in the window caught his attention. The woman had long, long dark hair that was deeper than the shadows. Her eyes were just as dark as her hair, and the photographer had caught a wicked gleam in them.

Those eyes made a man wonder.

Did the darkness still tease a man first thing in the morning when she was waking up in bed? Did they ever glow blind with passion, reckless, unthinking, unknowing? It might only be a photograph, but the camera had captured a part of her, and the gleam stayed there. A teasing Lolita, a brazen Delilah?

He stood and looked for a minute, happy for the anonymity of a busy street. Where no one cared if a man stood a little too long, or stared a little too hard.

Sam knew that face; a face he'd had on the show— once.

Mercedes Brooks.

It'd been over a year ago, and he'd pushed her from his mind, a typical show amidst hundreds of shows, but the photograph stirred up a visceral reaction that surprised him with both its appearance and its intensity.

Spurred on by an impulse that he didn't want to examine, Sam walked inside, picked up a book off the display, and started to read. He should've known it'd be a mistake, everything about her yelled 'mistake' but he wanted to know, and his eyes followed the evocative, blood-heating words:

He wasn't a man she'd ever see outside the bedroom, because his world wasn't hers, and she couldn't adapt to his, so they met in private, in the dark, and for a few hours, they would pretend.

She loved lying next to him, his body so much stronger and bigger than hers. Sometimes she would trail her fingers over his arms, following the ridges and dips, the curling hairs tickling the pads of her fingers. He had lovely arms that sheltered her, and kept her warm when the world was cold, cherished her when she felt unloved.

His body was built to pleasure her, with his big, hard, workman's hands. She loved when he rubbed them over her, slow at first, almost shy. He wore a ring on his right hand, cold silver that jarred when he rubbed it over the heated skin of her breasts. He would do that to her, and at first she thought it was an accident, but by the third time, she grew to love that ring, and the simple wanton pleasure of cold silver against a naked breast. Her breasts weren't the only place he teased. He liked to delve between her thighs, the ring pressing against hot, swollen flesh. A single touch that would pull her out of her skin, but never fast. Always slow, excruciatingly slow...

"Sam Porter?"

The voice jerked him out of that sensual place he'd just visited with his vivid imagination. He glanced down.

Quickly, he covered his crotch with the book and turned.

An older woman stood there, her eyes as curious as a kid's. She was bundled up in a wool cardigan, and carried a stack of books in her hands. "You're reading that?" she asked, the bright eyes dipping to the lurid cover.

Instantly, Sam put on his fan-face. "Oh, no. Just like to keep up with the state of the world."

She clucked her tongue, the faded red hair shaking in disapproval. He saw that look a lot. "Sad what's happening. Sometimes I think I'm just getting too old, that I don't understand the young. Sex, sex, sex. Seems like we get bombarded with it everywhere. Books, television, health insurance. Can you believe it, they're using sex to sell health insurance? You should put that on your show."

Carefully, unobtrusively, Sam replaced the Sex Book, then gave the woman an empathetic nod. "I think you're right. I'll talk to the writers."

The woman stared at the dark, shadowy cover displaying a man and a woman locked in a shameful, wicked, indecent embrace that look...

Sam looked harder.

...really inviting.

Time to cut to a commercial. "Listen, I need to run. There's never enough time, is there?"

The woman held out her hand, and Sam took it in his two. The women really liked that move, no matter the age.

"Watch us next week. We'll be heading out to San Francisco on Thursday and Friday."

The blue eyes grew wide. "Really?"

Sam smiled and gave her a confiding laugh. "New judge on the ninth circuit. I've got some questions. That's the way it starts. I always have questions."

Visibly she relaxed. "That's what I like about you.

You won't let anybody get away with anything. I won't miss it."

He signed an autograph for her, and then departed quickly, needing to escape from the wicked, gleaming eyes in the photograph. He was absolutely sure Mercedes Brooks was laughing at him. He ran a finger under the collar of his leather bomber jacket, feeling the sweat that had collected there. He swore under his breath, and shook his head, clearing the ghosts, and clearing the image of her.

O'Kelley's was a relief from the bookstore, casual, dim and loud. He scanned the room for the guys, spotting them at a table against the black-paneled wall, underneath the Harp beer sign. Bobby was a journalist who he'd bonded with when he was a political reporter for WNBC. The reason for the dinner was Tony Rapanelli, who, seven years ago, after a New Year's Eve party, had mistaken Bobby for a mugger, and tackled him in the middle of 8th Avenue. It was the start of a beautiful friendship.

However, now Tony was going through the last throes of a painful divorce, and it was sucking the life out of him slowly and surely. For three months, Sam and Bobby had been working with Tony, trying to cheer him up, trying to let him see life after a break-up, but Tony, who had been married for seventeen years, had two kids, two dogs, and one house in Jersey, hadn't even cracked a smile.

However, they were determined to keep trying.

Sam plastered a grin on his face. "Hey! Didn't mean to keep you guys waiting."

Robert stood and knocked his fist, an odd mix of formality and the street. Although he always wore a jacket,

Franco was half Puerto-Rican, half Italian and still carried around some of the old ways. "My man, how's things?"

"Eh," Sam answered, ordering a Diet Coke from the waitress.

He settled into a chair and grabbed the bowl of pretzels, the best he was going to manage for dinner.

Tony raised his glass. "To women."

Sam raised a brow. This was new. Maybe they were lucky, and Tony had gotten laid. In Sam's experience, sex always put a rosy spin on life.

"Today is Tony's anniversary," muttered Bobby, before Sam could get too carried away with excitement. "Listen, Tone, the wife has a friend. Now, she's not a stunner, but she's nice—"

The table broke out in groans. "And she got a boob job last year," he finished.

"Age?" asked Tony.

"Thirty-two."

"What's wrong with her?" he asked.

"Now, wait a minute," Sam interrupted. "Tony, you're thirty-seven. Absolutely nothing is wrong with you, and there's no reason to assume that there's a problem." Sam believed in fighting injustices wherever they occurred, even in his friends.

"Point taken," admitted Tony, and then turned back to Bobby. "So what's wrong with her?"

"Were you listening?" asked Sam. "There doesn't have to be anything wrong with her. Right, Bob?"

Bob got all shifty-eyed and Sam groaned. "Look, she's got this voice. Kinda Brooklyn."

"No, absolutely not," said Tony, using two syllables at the end, just like any good Long Islander would do.

"God, how do you plan on meeting any women if no one is good enough?"

Bobby laughed. "Spoken like the eternally single man that you are."

"I was married. Once." It'd been a long time ago, Sam thought to himself. He'd been young, she'd been young. "Mistakes were made. Life goes on."

"There's nothing wrong with marriage," answered Bobby.

"No, there's not," said Tony, reminding them all of why they were there.

Sam took another pretzel and munched happily. "You just got to get back on the horse. I'll take you to a club, you meet women, see them all nicely dressed, or undressed, and remind you of what you are."

"What's that?" asked Tony.

Sam smiled, wide and slow. "You're the rarest of the rare. A precious quantity to be savored and sipped, and tupped as often as you like. You're a single, heterosexual man in New York City."

He might as well have thrown him in front of a bus, for all the good it did. Tony attempted a smile. "I don't know that I can do this."

"Don't worry about it. I'll call around. We'll find the good places."

"I thought you had a girlfriend now," asked Bobby.

"Not anymore," said Sam, who was always very careful with his relationships. Shelia had been nice enough, but she wasn't The One. He hadn't met The One, and until he did, hey, he was a single heterosexual man in New York City.

* * * * *

Turn the page for a sneak preview of
IF I'D NEVER KNOWN YOUR LOVE
by
Georgia Bockoven

From the brand-new series
Harlequin Everlasting Love
Every great love has a story to tell. ™

There's no way for you to know this, Evan, but I haven't written to you for a few months. Actually, it's been almost a year. I had a hard time picking up a pen once more after we paid the second ransom and then received a letter saying it wasn't enough. I was so sure you were coming home that I took the kids along to Bogotá so they could fly home with you and me, something I swore I'd never do. I've fallen in love with Colombia and the people who've opened their hearts to me. But fear is a constant companion when I'm there. I won't ever expose our children to that kind of danger again.

I'm at a loss over what to do anymore, Evan. I've begged and pleaded and thrown temper tantrums with every official I can corner both here and at home. They've been incredibly tolerant and understanding, but in the end as ineffectual as the rest of us.

I try to imagine what your life is like now, what you do every day, what you're wearing, what you eat. I want to believe that the people who have you are misguided yet kind, that they treat you well. It's how I survive day to day. To think of you being mistreated hurts too much. If I picture you locked away somewhere and suffering, a weight descends on me that makes it almost impossible to get out of bed in the morning.

Your captors surely know you by now. They have to recognize what a good man you are. I imagine you working with their children, telling them that you have children, too, showing them the pictures you carry in your wallet. Can't the men who have you understand how much your children miss you? How can it not matter to them?

How can they keep you away from us all this time? Over and over, we've done what they asked. Are they oblivious to the depth of their cruelty? What kind of people are they that they don't care?

I used to keep a calendar beside our bed next to the peach rose you picked for me before you left. Every night I marked another day, counting how many you'd been gone. I don't do that any longer. I don't want to be reminded of all the days we'll never get back.

When I can't sleep at night, I tell you about my day. I imagine you hearing me and smiling over the details that make up my life now. I never tell you how defeated I feel at moments or how hard I work to hide it from everyone for fear they will see it as a reason to stop believing you are coming home to us.

And I couldn't tell you about the lump I found

in my breast and how difficult it was going through all the tests without you here to lean on. The lump was benign—the process reaching that diagnosis utterly terrifying. I couldn't stop thinking about what would happen to Shelly and Jason if something happened to me.

We need you to come home.

I'm worn down with missing you.

I'm going to read this tomorrow and will probably tear it up or burn it in the fireplace. I don't want you to get the idea I ever doubted what I was doing to free you or thought the work a burden. I would gladly spend the rest of my life at it, even if, in the end, we only had one day together.

You are my life, Evan.

I will love you forever.

* * * * *

Don't miss this deeply moving Harlequin Everlasting Love story about a woman's struggle to bring back her kidnapped husband from Colombia and her turmoil over whether to let go, finally, and welcome another man into her life.
IF I'D NEVER KNOWN YOUR LOVE
by Georgia Bockoven
is available March 27, 2007.

And also look for
THE NIGHT WE MET
by Tara Taylor Quinn,
a story about finding love
when you least expect it.

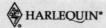

HARLEQUIN® *Romance®*

presents a brand-new trilogy by

PATRICIA THAYER

Rocky Mountain
B R I D E S

Three sisters come home to wed.

In April don't miss

Raising the Rancher's Family,

followed by

The Sheriff's Pregnant Wife,

on sale May 2007,

and

A Mother for the Tycoon's Child,

on sale June 2007.

Silhouette®

Romantic
SUSPENSE

Excitement, danger
and passion guaranteed!

USA TODAY bestselling author
Marie Ferrarella
is back with the second installment
in her popular miniseries,
*The Doctors Pulaski: Medicine
just got more interesting...*
DIAGNOSIS: DANGER is on sale
April 2007 from Silhouette®
Romantic Suspense (formerly
Silhouette Intimate Moments).

*Look for it wherever
you buy books!*

REQUEST YOUR FREE BOOKS!

2 FREE NOVELS PLUS 2 FREE GIFTS!

HARLEQUIN®

Blaze®

Red-hot reads!

YES! Please send me 2 FREE Harlequin® Blaze® novels and my 2 FREE gifts. After receiving them, if I don't wish to receive any more books, I can return the shipping statement marked "cancel." If I don't cancel, I will receive 6 brand-new novels every month and be billed just $3.99 per book in the U.S., or $4.47 per book in Canada, plus 25¢ shipping and handling per book and applicable taxes, if any*. That's a savings of at least 15% off the cover price! I understand that accepting the 2 free books and gifts places me under no obligation to buy anything. I can always return a shipment and cancel at any time. Even if I never buy another book from Harlequin, the two free books and gifts are mine to keep forever.

151 HDN EF3W   351 HDN EF3X

Name	(PLEASE PRINT)	
Address		Apt.
City	State/Prov.	Zip/Postal Code

Signature (if under 18, a parent or guardian must sign)

Mail to the **Harlequin Reader Service®**:
IN U.S.A.: P.O. Box 1867, Buffalo, NY 14240-1867
IN CANADA: P.O. Box 609, Fort Erie, Ontario L2A 5X3

Not valid to current Harlequin Blaze subscribers.

Want to try two free books from another line?
Call 1-800-873-8635 or visit www.morefreebooks.com.

* Terms and prices subject to change without notice. NY residents add applicable sales tax. Canadian residents will be charged applicable provincial taxes and GST. This offer is limited to one order per household. All orders subject to approval. Credit or debit balances in a customer's account(s) may be offset by any other outstanding balance owed by or to the customer. Please allow 4 to 6 weeks for delivery.

Your Privacy: Harlequin is committed to protecting your privacy. Our Privacy Policy is available online at www.eHarlequin.com or upon request from the Reader Service. From time to time we make our lists of customers available to reputable firms who may have a product or service of interest to you. If you would prefer we not share your name and address, please check here. ☐

HB07

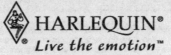

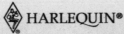

COMING NEXT MONTH

#315 COMING UNDONE Stephanie Tyler
There's a bad boy in camouflage knocking at Carly Winters's door, and she knows she's in trouble. The erotic fax that Jonathon "Hunt" Huntington's waving in her face—she can explain; how the buff Navy SEAL got ahold of it—she can't. But she sure wants to find out!

#316 SEX AS A SECOND LANGUAGE Jamie Sobrato
Lust in Translation, Bk. 1
Ariel Turner's sexual tour of Europe has landed her in Italy seeking the perfect Italian lover. But despite the friendliness of the locals, she's not having much luck. Until the day the very hot Marc Sorrella sits beside her. Could it be she's found the ideal candidate?

#317 THE HAUNTING Hope Tarr
Extreme
History professor Maggie Holliday's new antebellum home has everything she's ever wanted—including the ghost of Captain Ethan O'Malley, a Union soldier who insists Maggie's the reincarnation of his lost love. And after one incredibly sexual night in his arms, she's inclined to believe him....

#318 AT HIS FINGERTIPS Dawn Atkins
Doing it...Better! Bk. 3
When a fortune-teller predicts the return of a man from her past, Esmeralda McElroy doesn't expect Mitch Margolin. The sexy sizzle is still between them, but he's a lot more cautious than she remembers. Does this mean she'll have to seduce him to his senses?

#319 BAD BEHAVIOR Kristin Hardy
Sex & the Supper Club II, Bk. 3
Dominick Gordon can't believe it. He thinks his eyes are playing tricks on him when he spots the older, but no less beautiful, Delaney Phillips—it's been almost twenty years since they dated as teenagers. Still, Dom's immediate feelings show he's all man, and Delaney's all woman....

#320 ALL OVER YOU Sarah Mayberry
Secret Lives of Daytime Divas, Bk. 2
The last thing scriptwriter Grace Wellington wants is for the man of her fantasies to step into her life. But Mac Harrison, in his full, gorgeous glory, has done exactly that. Worse, they're now working together. That is, if Grace can keep her hands to herself!

www.eHarlequin.com   HBCNM0307